THE CORPSE
IN CACTUS

THE DETECTIVE MAGGIE REARDON SERIES

The Mosaic Murder
The Corpse in the Cactus

ALSO BY LONNI LEES

Crawlspace
Deranged

THE CORPSE IN CACTUS

LONNI LEES

A Detective Maggie Reardon Mystery

THE BORGO PRESS

Published by Wildside Press LLC.
www.wildsidebooks.com

CHAPTER ONE

The Darkening Sky

The Cactus Needle Bar wasn't a Tucson hot spot where people went to be noticed. It was quite the opposite. Tucked away on an industrial side street, it was recessed from the sidewalk, flanked by two large warehouses. Most of the letters on the neon sign had sputtered out long ago. The owner either didn't notice or didn't care.

The bar stretched the length of the dimly lit room, flanked by mostly empty bar stools. The floor was scattered with sawdust, the air filled with the aroma of stale beer and despair. A tall, young man sat at the far end, facing the wall and nursing his drink. A woman wore a face that told a story of too many years and too many drinks. She sat at the bar trying to make eye contact with the two men playing pool in hopes of not having to spend another night in an empty bed. The sound of clacking pool balls competed with the country music blaring from the jukebox.

An older man and a young woman sat at a table at the opposite corner. His eyes would dart uneasily around the room, then he'd take another slug of his drink and lower his head as she leaned into him. His spending what little money they had on alcohol bothered her. Even though it helped calm him it just wasn't right. Not when there was no food in their stomachs. She knew that much but said nothing. Keeping her thoughts to herself was the safest. He made the rules and she obeyed them. For the most part anyway. That was just how it was.

The pool players finished their game. The one with the beer belly walked over to the bar for a refill and tossed a pick-up line staler than his breath toward the woman on the bar stool. She smiled as he eased closer to her. The other man, unshaven with an awkward gait and jangling spurs on his boots, walked over to the table where the couple sat in the shadows. Ignoring the man, he smiled down at the young woman and tipped his Stetson hat, reaching out his hand. A sad song played on the jukebox, perfect for dancing and holding a warm body close to his.

"Would you like to dance?" he asked.

She was afraid to make eye contact, instead looking over nervously to the man sitting beside her. He lifted his head, eyes glaring at the man with an ice cold expression that made him take a backwards step.

"I apologize if I was rude. Would you mind if I dance with your daughter?"

He rose to his feet, spilling his drink in the process as he reached over and grabbed the man by his collar and twisting it tightly against his throat. "That's my wife," he said shoving the man backwards, his Stetson falling to the floor. "She's hands off."

The tall, young man at the far end of the bar turned at the sound of the commotion, then turned again to face the wall.

The young woman rose and rushed over to her husband, grabbing his arm as he clenched his fist ready to hit the guy.

"Don't honey," she said. "People are looking. You don't want to draw attention."

The pool player gasped for breath and coughed as he picked his hat up off the floor. He debated whether to fight, but the look in the man's eyes was bat guano crazy and he thought better of it. Besides, there was no point in brawling with some old guy bent on flexing his beer muscles.

"I didn't mean to offend you," he said politely, dusting off his hat and turning toward the bar. What was that young thing doing with an old nut job anyway? Those creepy eyes spelled nothing but trouble and he hadn't come to the Cactus Needle cruising for trouble. He walked over to where his friend sat with the drunk woman and took the barstool at her other side, draping his arm across her shoulder. After all, what were friends for if not for sharing?

The young woman talked her husband back into his seat and slid into the chair next to his.

"I could kill him," he said, the words hissing through clenched teeth like a rattlesnake ready to strike.

"Shhhh. It's just the devil trying to get hold of you, honey." She reached over and placed his empty glass upright. She motioned the bartender for a refill, then leaned over and lay her head against his shoulder.

"It's okay, baby. He meant no harm."

She gently rubbed the back of his neck, calming him down. The bartender walked over and sat the fresh drink on the table. "Everything okay here, sport?"

He reached for his drink, took a gulp, and said nothing.

He folded his arms around her.

Way too tightly.

But she knew better than to pull away from him.

* * * *

Dark clouds filled the late afternoon sky, promising to end months of Arizona drought. Steam rose from the ground as the first drops of rain danced across the hot blacktop and pinged onto the hoods of parked squad cars and unmarked vehicles. In the cactus beds that edged the sidewalk in front of the police station, rivulets were sucked hungrily into the cracked, dry earth. The aroma of creosote filled the air, heralding the beginning of a Tucson monsoon.

Detective Maggie Reardon crossed the parking lot, paused, then tilted her head upward. Rain splashed across her face and into her eyes. Every drop, as it trickled painfully across the swelling and bruises, reminded her of the violent encounter with her enraged ex-boyfriend. And yet, every drop of water felt as if it were cleansing her entire being. She was tired, exhausted both physically and emotionally. The murder at the Mosaic Gallery was solved, but instead of feeling victorious it gnawed at her insides. When Barbara Atwell, the gallery owner who had killed her husband, was walked away in handcuffs all that Maggie felt was empathy and a sense of defeat. But murder is murder and she'd done her job. That's what she was paid to do and why she'd become a cop in the first place. Now the court would decide Barbara's fate in a legal crap-shoot, lawyer against lawyer. Maggie's fingers traced the ache along her jaw and throbbing, swollen lips. She knew her feelings were colored by the memory of her own attack, but if it were her decision she'd have let the woman walk right out of the interrogation room and out the front door.

She knew that Barbara Atwell could just as easily have been herself.

The rain soaked Maggie's hair, flattening the short auburn spikes against her head. She pushed them back from where they clung to her forehead, then reached into her pocket. Her heart did a familiar skip-jump as she pulled out her cell phone and punched in the number. Rocco La Crosse had been one of many suspects in the case, so she'd fought her attraction to him, as well as his tactful advances. But that was finally yesterday's news. The case was closed and she hoped it wasn't too late. She debated hanging up. He might not be interested, especially when he found out she'd arrested his friend Barbara. Or maybe the attraction had fizzled before it ever started. It wasn't as if she'd encouraged him.

As she continued debating with herself, a husky, soft voice answered at the other end.

Just hearing him speak made her want to reach through the phone and hug the big teddy bear.

She braced herself for rejection before she spoke.

"Hello Rocco," she said.

"Who's this?"

Announcing herself as Detective Reardon would sound so formal, so indifferent. "This is Maggie," she said. "If you're still interested, I'm ready for that cup of coffee."

She stood in the rain, inhaling deeply as she waited for his response.

It came quickly. She listened to his voice, low and soft.

"Sure, that's just a few blocks from my house," she replied. "About fifteen minutes? I'll be the one that looks like a wet Irish setter."

She closed the cell phone and smiled. It looked like the day might end on a high note after all.

She shoved the phone into her purse and fished for her car keys.

"Detective Reardon!"

Maggie turned to see Adrian Velikson standing in the rain, waving frantically from where she stood at the entrance to the Police Department. At a distance she looked even shorter and wider than she did up close. Her usual bulldog demeanor looked downright defeated. Maggie's heart went out to her. Why Adrian would even want to speak to her was unfathomable. Maggie had just booked Adrian's lover for murder despite Adrian having confessed to the murder herself. Maggie had to be tops on the woman's enemy list.

"Detective Reardon," the woman repeated.

"Stay put!" Maggie yelled over the sound of the downpour. "I'll be right there."

She opened the car door, got in and shoved the key into the ignition. The engine made a grinding sound, then kicked in. She turned on the windshield wipers, threw the car into drive and maneuvered through the puddles to where Adrian stood. Maggie reached across and opened the passenger side door.

"Get in before you drown," she said.

A gust of wind nearly tore off the door as Adrian got into the car. Her rain soaked bottom made a squeaking sound as denim slid across vinyl. She pulled with both hands at the door until it slammed shut with a creak and a thud.

"I assume you don't want to talk to me about the weather," said Maggie as she pulled the car to the curb.

Adrian's bottom lip quivered and Maggie couldn't tell if it was rain or tears that trickled down her cheeks. Probably both. The woman looked down as she fidgeted with her stubby, calloused fingers, but said nothing.

The two of them sat in silence as they watched the rhythmic sway of windshield wipers against glass. One rubber strip waved loosely, flapping noisily as it tried to keep up with its undamaged partner. I really need to get those replaced, Maggie thought, trying to keep her mind on anything but what might come out of Adrian's mouth. It wouldn't be the first time that she'd been verbally skewered, but this time she had no smart-mouthed retort. The woman had been through an emotional ringer and the last thing Maggie wanted to do was add to it any more than she already had.

The first monsoon rain stopped as suddenly as it had begun.

The silence swallowed them as they watched the steam rising from the ground. A ray of sunshine leaked from between the clouds and dripped down onto the scattered puddles making them sparkle like gold dust.

Adrian finally spoke. "I don't know what to do," she said. "I'm lost. Could you just give me a ride back to the gallery? I need to get my thoughts together."

"I'm on my way to meet Rocco. Why don't you come along? Rocco needs to know what's happened and I'd be more comfortable with you there. It might help soften the blow. Besides, you look like you could use a hot cup of coffee."

"I'd completely forgotten! He has no idea that Barbara's in jail, let alone that she killed Armando." She looked over at Maggie and they locked eyes. "This isn't going to be easy for either of us."

"Rocco always knows what to do. You've said that more than once," Maggie said as she watched her fantasy of finally being alone with him fly out the window. There was no way he'd want to have anything to do with her now. What had she been thinking? She'd be nothing more than "bad cop" in his eyes. She sighed, not looking forward to closing the last chapter on what might have been. The bottom line was always the same. She was a cop first, just one reason her love life wavered endlessly between disastrous and non-existent.

Maggie pulled the car onto the street and headed toward the coffee shop. And Rocco La Crosse. She reassured Adrian as best she could. Despite facing first degree murder there were other options that could work in Barbara's favor. The judiciary system was a game that depended upon the players as well as blind luck. Lady Justice wore a blindfold for a reason. At best, a good lawyer could plead down the charges. She'd seen them do it enough times when the perp deserved the chair. They could certainly do it when the accused had, if not good reason, one that could feasibly be stretched to self-defense. If faced with a sympathetic jury the odds could improve tenfold, giving Barbara a chance to walk away with time served. Or she could spend the rest of her life behind bars. The tension in Adrian's body relaxed as they pulled into the parking lot of the coffee shop. The lot was nearly empty so she was able to pull into a spot near the door. As they walked toward the entrance Maggie spotted Rocco's Victory motorcycle parked in a far corner of the lot, beads of water glistening on its chrome.

"It looks like he beat us here," she said, using her back to push open the coffee shop door, then motioning with a nod for Adrian to enter.

The two women looked around the sparsely peopled room and spotted him at a far booth. He looked up. In a split second his expression went from puzzlement to disappointment, followed by a welcoming smile as he rose to greet them.

"My two favorite ladies," he said. "What a nice surprise."

Adrian ran to him.

She was crying again.

"Nothing can be that bad," he said, holding her.

"Nothing could be worse."

"There, there. Sit down and tell your uncle Rocco all about it."

Adrian slid into the booth and he sat down next to her. His hair and scraggly, dark beard were wet from rain and his damp tee-shirt clung to him, accentuating his round belly.

As she sat down, Maggie felt like an outsider and wanted to run to the nearest exit.

Adrian's sobbing drew attention from a couple sitting at the counter. The man spun around on his stool and looked in their direction. The woman with him looked over her shoulder, straining to hear their conversation.

"Turn around and mind your own business," Maggie snapped.

Embarrassed, they turned back to their plates.

"Sorry," Maggie said to Rocco. "It's been a lousy day. And you, you look as soaked as we do. Whatever possessed you to ride your motorcycle in the middle of a monsoon?"

"When I left the house the sky was clear. I was half-way down the hill when the clouds exploded."

"Why didn't you turn back and get the van?"

"And be late meeting you for that cup of coffee? I've waited long enough."

So far it didn't look as if his interest had waned. Maggie smiled, her swollen lip causing her to wince. Well, she might as well cut to the chase and see what he thinks then. Just get it over with and move on.

She braced herself. "I'm afraid Adrian and I are the bearers of bad news."

"Her waterworks gave me a clue. What's going on?" He put his arm around Adrian and hugged her close to him.

There was an awkward silence as Maggie tried to form the words. She looked pleadingly at Adrian, hoping she would speak first.

"It's Barbara," Adrian finally said, choking on the words. "They've arrested her for murdering Armando."

Her tears were starting up again.

"Barbara? Why in the world would Barbara want to kill her husband?"

"It's complicated," said Maggie. "You know those ugly little statues he was selling at the gallery? All the artists wondered how he managed to sell so many, right?"

Rocco nodded. "Some tastes definitely run to the tacky."

"Well, they were pretty special after all. It seems that he was using them to smuggle cocaine."

"You're kidding me."

"Barbara discovered what he was up to."

"All her hard work building a reputation and that rat was willing to ruin everything," Adrian chimed in.

"She must have been furious," said Rocco. "I'd have been."

"Not as angry as he was at having been found out," said Maggie. "Anyway, things escalated and he was shoving her around and threatening her."

"That's what happened to Belinda's goddess statue," said Adrian.

"I don't get it," he said.

"She picked it up and hit him over the head with it."

"Sounds like self-defense to me," he said.

"It's not that simple," said Maggie.

"Why not? She was protecting herself."

"Problem is," Maggie continued, "his back was turned at the time."

"A woman against a stronger man? It's like bringing a slingshot to a gunfight. It should be a slam-dunk."

"We can only hope so."

"I did everything I could," Adrian said, spilling out the story as fast as she could. "I didn't have a clue she'd killed Armando, not until today. So I told Detective Reardon that I killed him. I couldn't let her go to jail, I just couldn't. I could handle it, but not Barbara. Maggie took me to police headquarters and everything was going fine. Until Barbara showed up. I told her to shut up and go home but she just stood there and confessed to everything and I couldn't stop her."

Rocco looked stunned as he silently toyed with the large silver earring that dangled from his earlobe. He looked at Adrian, then at Maggie, then leaned back in the booth and exhaled loudly.

"I still can't believe it. It was Barbara?"

"Maybe it's best that I leave you two to talk," said Maggie as she squirmed in her seat. She slid across and rose, "I really don't belong here."

"Please, sit," said Rocco.

"You don't get it," she said. "I feel like a friend and an enemy and…"

Rocco reached a tattooed arm across the table, motioning her to sit.

"You're guilty of what, exactly? Doing your job? We consider you a friend. An unlikely one maybe, but a friend. I'm sure you agree with me, don't you Adrian?"

Adrian hesitated, then nodded.

"As strange as it may seem," he continued, "we've come to think of you as one of the pack. Please, sit down."

"Under the circumstances, it's a bit of an uneasy friendship, don't you think?"

"Who ever said life was going to be easy? Now sit."

Reluctantly, Maggie sat down and watched as Rocco lifted his coffee cup with one hand and held up two fingers with the other, motioning the waitress. The old broad looked like she'd been around since the place opened decades ago, just as boring and tired and worn as her surroundings. She took her time bringing over two more coffee mugs and filling them for Adrian and Maggie. Adrian took a long draw, then let out an animal noise as the coffee burned along her tongue and throat.

"Holy—"

"Patient as ever, I see," said Rocco.

Tears ran down her cheeks. "I have to do something for Barbara," she said. "I need to get her a lawyer and somehow fight this thing. I don't know how I'll ever come up with a retainer, much less court costs and…"

"Am I your friend?" he said.

"Y'yes."

"Do you rib me about being a trust fund baby?"

She lowered her eyes, ashamed, and nodded.

"It has its advantages," he said. "You don't have to worry about a thing."

"But…"

"Not financially anyway. My family has the best law firm in Tucson on permanent retainer. I'm sure they've got someone who can handle this."

"You would do that for us?"

"That's what friends are for."

"Oh, my God," said Maggie as a thought hit her. "Your lawyers might just end up pulling double duty!"

"What?"

"Adrian, you confessed to a murder you didn't commit."

"So? I was protecting Barbara."

"There's a chance you could be charged with obstruction of justice."

Adrian groaned.

"Well," said Rocco, "it looks like those crafty lawyers might finally start earning their keep."

"But—"

"Don't worry about a thing. I'll make calls first thing in the morning. Coming from a powerful family has it's advantages and it's about time I started using some of that La Crosse clout."

"You're my favorite rebel," said Adrian. "Do you know how much I love you?"

"Not enough to consider going straight," he laughed.

Maggie was starting to relax. She lifted her mug to her swollen mouth and took a painful sip. An ear shattering clap of thunder caused the three of them to jump, followed by another. And another. She set down her mug and looked out the window. The rain beat violently against the windowpane and streamed down the glass like a raging river.

"I guess we should call it a day," said Rocco, grabbing the bill. "The tab's on me."

"You can't possibly ride your motorcycle in this," said Maggie.

"Hey, I'm the tough guy, remember?"

"Don't be silly," she answered, rising from the booth. She reached into her pocket and pulled out her keys, fidgeting with them. She pulled one off the key ring and handed it to him as he and Adrian slid out of the booth. "I'm only two blocks from here. Put your bike in my garage, let yourself in, and I'll meet you there after I drive Adrian back to the gallery."

There was a twinkle in Adrian's eye as she looked at Maggie, then at Rocco, then back at Maggie.

"I couldn't impose," he said.

"Do you remember where I live?"

"How could I forget? I came to your rescue, remember?"

"Okay then. It'll give you a chance to dry out until the rain lets up."

Maggie and Adrian ran for the car as Rocco headed to the cash register.

As Maggie drove to the gallery, Adrian talked non-stop, adrenaline rushing through her veins like a runaway virus. She was high on optimism knowing that, once again, Rocco knew what to do.

"He can do it, I know he can," she said. "If anyone can make this nightmare go away it's Rocco."

Maggie pulled the car up in front of the gallery.

"Do you really think they'll charge me with something?" she asked.

"Not if I can help it. But remember, I can only do so much."

"I was only trying to help Barbara," she said.

"You committed a crime, whether they want to call it obstruction of justice or abetting. What you did was stupid."

"People in love do stupid things."

"Tell me about it." Maggie had her own history of being stupid in the name of love.

Once again tears welled in Adrian's eyes.

"Not the water works again," Maggie said. "All that crying isn't going to help one iota."

"Armando was attacking her. That's got to count for something."

Adrian exited the car and Maggie watched as she raced through the pouring rain, through the archway to the Mosaic Gallery and up the back stairs that led to Barbara's and her apartment.

The wind whipped around the car as she stepped on the gas and headed towards home. And a waiting Rocco La Crosse.

CHAPTER TWO

Pretty in Peach

Detective Maggie Reardon drove down the darkened street and pulled into her driveway. The rain was finally letting up. Rocco La Crosse stood at the window of her house in the soft lamp light, waiting. Maggie wasn't used to anything waiting for her at the end of the day except her cat. It felt odd, awkward. But on some level it felt pretty darn good. She wondered if she was finally getting it right or if she was just setting herself up for more disappointment. The two of them were polar opposites on so many levels, but the attraction was undeniable. At least for her. Maybe it was nothing more than hormones and chemistry. That had been her mistake more than once. They held a double wham-my that could toss logic and common sense right out the window and turn an intelligent person into a fool. But it could be something more. Maybe. The best she could do was dive in head first and play it out. See where it headed. Or where it hit the concrete wall. Sometimes that impulsive approach worked. Sometimes it was disastrous. Her instincts rarely let her down. Except where affairs of the heart were concerned.

She turned off the ignition, exited the car, and headed for her front door. It opened when she hit the top step, Rocco greeting her with his generous smile. He bowed, a most unlikely knight in shining armor.

"*Entre vous*, m'lady," he said with a sweep of his arm as he held her cat Prowler with the other. Prowler was purring up a storm, so unlike the ungrateful monster. Apparently Rocco could work his rough-edged charm on beasts as well as the ladies. She walked into the living room and heard Rocco close the door behind them. Maggie felt as awkward as a girl greeting her first prom date. But there was no father there to scrutinize him. No wise parents to put on the brakes when she was headed in the wrong direction. Her heart ached as she thought of how much she still missed them. And time hadn't eased the loss.

Staying in the home where they had raised her wasn't the best idea, but she couldn't let go. She still sat in the over-stuffed chair where her father read his newspaper. She still used the dishes and silverware that had been among their wedding gifts. She still used their old, battered toaster. In some small way those things kept them close.

"I hope you don't mind that I fed the cat," said Rocco. "He's pushy."

"That's an understatement."

Maggie undid her gun belt and tossed it onto the side table by her chair, nearly knocking over the lamp. "I'd offer you coffee, but I'm caffeined out. How about a drop of Irish?"

"To warm the cockles of me cold, cold heart? Sounds great."

Maggie walked into the kitchen and removed two glasses from the cupboard. She reached across the counter for the bottle of Old Bush-mill's, uncapped it to pour, then changed her mind. Tonight she'd need more than a few. When she walked back into the living room, bottle in one hand and glasses held in the other, Rocco was still standing, holding Prowler.

"You look uncomfortable. Why don't you toss the cat? Sit down and relax." She poured his whiskey and handed him the glass.

"Oh, did you want ice? I drink mine straight up, as the Celtic gods intended."

Why did she always jabber on when she was nervous, she wondered, taking a deep breath.

He looked down at his clothes.

"I'm still wet," he said. "I don't want to mess up your furniture. And no, no ice is fine." He scratched the cat behind its ear. "Toss the cat?"

"Unlike some of us, he always lands on his feet."

Rocco lowered Prowler gently to the floor and reached for his glass. The cat protested and walked a way in a huff.

This is getting awkward, Maggie thought as she looked at him standing there soaked to the skin.

"Get those clothes off and I'll toss them in the dryer."

He smiled.

"No, no, no. Just go into the bathroom and hand them out to me. I'm not suggesting…"

"I never thought for a minute," he winked and sat down his drink.

Maggie led him to the bathroom, went back to the living room and filled her glass. Things certainly weren't going as she'd imagined, but reality always trumps daydream. She thought back to the night she'd fallen asleep against his chest. How he'd been there for her after her attack. How comforting it had felt. She gulped some whiskey and let it slide down her throat, smooth and sweet as wild honey. A bit of liquid courage. The timing was off. After all, she'd just wound things up with the ex boyfriend who'd stalked and assaulted her. Marty was sitting in jail where he belonged. He was barely out the door when she welcomed in Rocco La Crosse. Not smart. She needed time to sort things out, figure out where she'd gone wrong before jumping into a repeat performance with this man she hardly knew. Not to mention she'd just arrested his friend. Things hadn't even begun and already it was too complicated and making her head spin. She didn't like complications. She took another sip of whiskey, reached for her smokes and slid one out of the pack. She raised it to her lips, lit it and inhaled deeply. Soft rain tapped against the window.

"Detective Reardon?"

She placed her cigarette in the ashtray, rose and followed his voice down the hall. The bathroom door was slightly ajar. A tattooed arm reached out, clothes in hand.

"I'll throw these in the dryer," she said, taking them. "They'll be ready in no time."

"There's a problem."

"What?"

"I don't have anything to put on…and I doubt you want me to come out like this. I don't think you're ready for the shock."

"Not much shocks me, but I'd prefer you wrapped." For now anyway, she thought.

"Should I wait in here or just throw a towel around myself?"

"Uh, um" she stuttered. "Let me think." She mentally took stock of her wardrobe. Rocco was a large man and wouldn't fit into even her baggiest t-shirt. Or anything else she had. I shouldn't have given all my father's clothes away, she thought, but even they would have been too small to wrap around his generous girth.

"Uh, there's a robe on the hook," she said. "On the back of the door…if you think you're man enough to handle it."

She could hear him laughing as she headed to the laundry room, Prowler trotting close at her heels. Maggie tossed his clothes into the dryer and Prowler jumped in before she could close the door. He fought and growled as she pulled him out, then slammed the door and pressed the button.

"Ornery little bugger," she scolded. "I should have you declawed."

Prowler beat her back to the living room and was racing toward Rocco when Maggie walked into the room. She wrapped her arms around her stomach and burst into laughter. Rocco stood there, wrapped in her faded peach chenille robe. It barely fit, and he had discreetly twisted it around so that the gap exposed his hip rather than falling open in the front. The sash barely fit around his middle, but he'd managed it into a knot. The cat reached up, hooking his claws into the fabric. Rocco grabbed at the worn robe before Prowler managed to rearrange it. Maggie couldn't stop laughing.

"What," he said. "You don't find me irresistible?"

Maggie looked at the burly bear of a figure and tried to catch her breath.

"It's just that," she gasped, "you look so pretty in peach."

Rocco reached down and unhooked Prowler's claws and as he lifted him, the hem of the robe rose to a dangerous height. He pulled it back down and smiled at her.

"Sorry about that," he said. "And stop laughing. After all, you've only yourself to blame for my wardrobe."

"Okay, okay. I'm just kidding you. I think the combination of soft fabric against hairy legs makes quite a fashion statement. You look really—adorable."

"I've been called a lot of things, but never adorable." He walked over to the couch and sat down, reaching for his drink as the cat settled on his lap. "I'm ready for some drink," he said, downing his whiskey and refilling the glass.

"You're a good sport, Rocco. I like that." She walked over to the stereo, shuffled through cd's and shoved one into the slot. The mellow notes of John Coltrain's tenor sax playing Blue Train blended with the sound of the rain. She walked back to the couch and sat next to Rocco.

She reached toward the ashtray where her cigarette had burned out. She pulled out another one from the pack and lit it.

Did she detect a flash of disapproval?

"Hey, I'm not politically correct. I need one, so deal with it," she said defensively as she lit it. She took a deep drag, but was careful to blow the smoke away from him. "Even a cop is entitled to one good vice. And this is mine."

"No need to be defensive. Relax. You're wound up tighter than a ball of rubber bands."

"It's that obvious?"

"If it's because of me…"

She poured some more whiskey into her glass and took a drink.

"You know, even with that black eye and swollen lip I think you're cute as a button," he said. Then added: "I just don't get how a man could do something like that."

"I have a knack for pissing people off."

"He was a brute. And he damn near killed you."

"It's behind me and I'm still breathing."

"You're a tough cookie, Maggie Reardon."

Prowler sandwiched himself between them.

"He's here to visit me, you scoundrel, not you."

The cat let out a low growl between his purrs and glared at her as he returned to Rocco's lap.

"You've got competition," he said as he stroked the cat's jet black fur.

* * * *

The rain had stopped. The last bar had closed for the night as the man and girl walked side by side down the wet sidewalk, neon reflecting like a dark rainbow beneath their feet. Every few steps the man lost his footing and the girl grabbed his arm to steady his balance. He walked with the gait of a middle-aged man, she with the spring of youth, yet their steps were synchronized as if they'd been together a lifetime. She looked as if she were dressed in her mother's or big sister's hand-me-downs. The hem of her too long prairie skirt dragged along the concrete, collecting mud and debris in its wake. The streets were empty but for a few stragglers feeling their way through the dark or seeking out their prey. The man and girl whispered and laughed as they walked. As the man stopped, a shadowy figure stepped into the darkness of a doorway, remaining unobserved as the man turned and looked behind him.

"What's the matter?" the girl asked.

"I think we're being followed," he said.

"You've been saying that for a week and I'm sick of it. Why do you always think somebody's following us?"

"I can't shake the feeling."

"Every time you get that feeling you make us pack up and move."

"It's for our safety."

"Safety from what exactly?"

"I'm not sure," he slurred.

"You're drunk. And besides, I like it here and I want to stay. Just once can't we settle in instead of living like gypsies?"

"We'll see."

You like it here, don't you?"

"I suppose."

"It doesn't snow. It doesn't freeze."

"It sure can rain though," he said looking up at the black sky. "To-night we should've taken the car, even if it is running on fumes."

"It rains maybe twice a year here, right? The rest of the time they say it's pure sunshine. I don't think it gets better than this."

"We'll see, sweetness. We'll see."

"That's what you said in Albuquerque. That's what you said every-where. Just once I'd like to stay in a place long enough to make friends. To feel like I belong somewhere."

The man tensed the muscles that crossed his shoulders, then relaxed them. She was making him nervous. She'd always done as she was told, never questioning his wisdom or motives. But lately he'd noticed a subtle change. Not only had she begun asking questions, but in her meek way it was almost as if she were trying to make demands. He didn't want to settle anywhere. It wasn't safe. And her new attitude wasn't safe either. It could put them both in jeopardy.

There was one solution but he didn't want to go there. He loved her. He always had. And she loved him, so killing her was out of the question. Somehow he'd have to reel her back in, make her realize again that he was always right and knew what was best for them both.

Her total submission was essential for their survival.

"You belong with me. Aren't I your best friend? Haven't I always looked out for you?"

"You always have," she said. There was a passiveness to her voice, a weary undertone as if she'd said those words a thousand times before.

The man looked behind him one more time before they continued to walk into the night. The stranger stepped out from his hiding place, careful to stay a safe distance behind them. He watched as they turned the corner onto Miracle Mile, a misnamed street filled with run-down motels. A human graffiti of derelicts, losers and addicts marred the landscape, crawling along the broken sidewalk like rats, leaving a trail of defeat in their wake.

Long and lean, the man in the shadows continued to tail them and watched as they turned into a cheap motel. A glaring neon flamingo left over from the 1950's sputtered and buzzed overhead. He watched as the man pulled the motel key from his jeans pocket and inserted it into the lock. He watched as they entered and closed the gaudy pink door to room twelve behind them.

The tall man turned and walked away. He had to be sure. He'd been searching for a very long time and he had to be absolutely sure. He turned up the side street to where his car was parked, got in and drove back, parking across the street from the run-down motel. And waited.

Detective Maggie Reardon and Rocco La Crosse sat comfortably on the couch listening to the mellow jazz and soft rainfall and the purring cat. He still wore her bathrobe. They drained their glasses in unison and sat them on the coffee table.

"Refill?" Maggie asked.

"I'd better stop," he said. "I'm getting buzzed."

"Works better than Valium," she said. "I haven't felt this relaxed in a long time."

"I hope it's from the company and not the liquid courage."

She looked at the nearly empty bottle and in her best imitation of an Irish brogue said: "Aye, Mr. La Crosse, just call it a weakness."

"I think we're both a bit nervous tonight," he said. "Getting to know each other better is the hard part, but Maggie, first time I laid eyes on you I felt something. It's hard to explain really. You were standing there wearing that gun belt with your disheveled hair and serious demeanor and all I could think was…"

"You've got a thing for girls with guns? You must have loved Helen Mirren in Red."

"Totally hot," he said.

The bong, bong, bong of the mantle clock interrupted his thoughts as it slowly announced the midnight hour. Nearly in unison, the dryer buzzed. His clothes were dry.

"Saved by the bells," said Maggie.

"It can wait."

Rocco reached across the cat to get closer to her. He wrapped an arm across her shoulder and she instinctively leaned toward him. Prowler let out a soft growl as Maggie elbowed him onto the floor.

"He thinks he's our chaperone," she said.

"You don't need protection. Not from me."

And she believed him.

Rocco held a hand softly against her cheek and tilted her face toward his. Their lips met.

Maggie jerked away.

"I'm sorry," he said. "I'm moving too fast."

"No," she said, groaning as she held a hand to her swollen lip. "It's just that—that my mouth still hurts and it felt like I was kissing a prickly pear cactus!"

Rocco looked at her bruises and felt foolish. "I'm so sorry," he said. "I got caught up in the moment. I wasn't thinking. It's hard to think straight when I'm around you."

"Our timing hasn't been so hot, has it?"

"An exercise in obstacles."

"Maybe it's an omen."

"Awe, c'mon Maggie. You sound so…Irish. It's not like the banshee is wailing outside the window."

She stiffened. "I didn't know the arrogant French knew about banshees."

"I read a lot."

"So I've observed," she said, thinking of the bursting bookshelves in his home up in the foothills.

"Hey, are you looking to start a war or what?"

"Is your next crack going to be about a quick Irish temper?"

"Maggie, Maggie, just relax."

"I'm nervous. And I hurt."

"That s.o.b. really did a number on you."

"And I'm sorry that you're taking the brunt of it. It's just that between you and me and the murder and Barbara and everything else it's so complicated."

"It doesn't have to be. Besides, some things are worth waiting for."

Maggie rose from the couch and went to the laundry room, returning with an armful of warm, dry clothes and handing them to Rocco. He trotted down the hall and into the bathroom, Prancer following close behind and bolting into the room before he could close him out.

He returned the peach bathrobe to the hook on the door and dressed. When he returned to the living room Maggie was standing by the front door.

"The rain's let up and it's getting late. We should call it a night."

At times she's so abrupt and blunt, he thought, and other times she's impossible to read.

"You're right," he said as he walked over and stood next to her.

"About that kiss…" she said.

"Out of line, I know."

"No," she said, moving closer to him. "What I wanted to say was, that if you're game, I'd like to give it another try."

He leaned forward and kissed her gently on the forehead.

"When the time is right," he said.

CHAPTER THREE

Messing Up Paradise

"Why can't I go out?" the girl pleaded, closing the motel room draperies to block out the morning sun and anything else that might want to peer in. "I just want to go for a walk."

"We can walk together when I get back."

There was no sense arguing with him. Even when she disagreed with him, he always knew what was best.

"Where are you going?" she asked.

"I need to find a big box store, some building supply place, and look for day work."

"I could come."

"And stand out there with the illegals and junkies? It could be dangerous."

"I hadn't thought of that."

"That's why it's important I do the thinking for both of us. I'm your husband and it's my job to protect you. And right now I need work to pay the front desk."

"It'd be nice if you found a real job. You know, so we can settle down."

"This is cash in pocket, no questions asked."

The man opened the door and looked back at her. She was soft and pretty with chestnut brown hair, but those pale blue eyes never stopped reminding him of a time and place best forgotten. He'd succeeded in keeping her innocent of the outside world. She had no world beyond him, but it was getting increasingly difficult as she grew older.

"And don't turn on the tv. It's the devil's box of lies and deceptions."

"I promise."

He couldn't be with her every minute, so he suspected there were times that she did turn it on. Because somehow, no matter how careful he was, she saw things that made her ask questions. So he lied and she believed him. The only truth she knew was what he told her and he needed to keep it that way. She was his world and he was hers and that was how it had to be.

And that was how it needed to remain.

So far he'd been successful in keeping them both safe, even if it did mean endless moves from place to place. Maybe some day he could grant her wish and settle somewhere, but not yet.

Not until that uneasy feeling went away.

"Lock the door behind me," he said. He walked back to where she stood and hugged her. "Everything will be fine. And I promise we'll take a nice walk when I get back, okay?"

When he left she locked the door just as she was told.

"No tv," she mumbled to herself as she walked across the room.

The tall, young man watched from across the street as the man in the plaid flannel shirt exited the motel room and got into his old green Chevy. He followed at a safe distance and pulled over, waiting, when the man stopped to gas up. When the man pulled into the lot of the building supply, the man parked a few rows behind him and watched as he walked across the parking lot and joined a small group of men standing at the far corner. He waited a long time, watching, as one by one the men would get into cars or trucks. A red pick-up, it's back filled with lumber, pulled up and he watched as the man walked over and spoke with the person behind the wheel. After a short exchange, the man in the worn flannel shirt got in and they drove away.

The young man returned to his car. Weary from another sleepless night, he stretched out across the front seat and slept. It had been a long journey and he'd learned patience. He would wait for as long as it took for the man to return to his car.

He would wait as long as need be to figure things out.

To be sure.

To be absolutely certain.

* * * *

"Normal? How can you expect me to act like things are normal? There's nothing about this whole situation that's normal!"

At The Mosaic Gallery, Adrian Velikson questioned Rocco La Crosse as he sat across the desk from her.

"I talked to Friedman first thing this morning and the wheels are turning. He didn't appreciate my waking him out of a dead sleep, but that's what he's getting paid for."

"Okay, so you can flex those money muscles when you have to, but he'll need to be one hell of a lawyer to get Barbara out of this mess."

"You know I don't like using the La Cross family's clout. I've never been comfortable there, not even as a kid. I was born the black sheep with the silver spoon. But our law firm is the best in Tucson. Hell, it's the best in Arizona. The time has come to put my feelings aside so I can help."

"But still."

"At a time like this having the right connections comes in handy."

"I can't be so positive." She pushed her chair back and rose, placing her fists stubbornly on her broad hips. "How can you see sunshine when I see disaster? You're not realistic."

"I'd like to pretend we live in a magnanimous world, but we don't. It's corrupt and it's tainted. That's realistic. Our Mosaic family is the closest we'll come to how we'd like the world to be, but even that falls short."

"But we try."

"And we'll keep on trying, but people aren't perfect. We accept them as they are, but sometimes we're forced to play hardball and this is one of those times."

"What do you mean?" Adrian sat back down in her chair with a thud.

"I'm not a lawyer and I can't fight this alone. Listen Adrian, Friedman owes me. That's how things work in the real world. Your burning incense and singing Kumbayah all day long won't change that. You'd be surprised what gets accomplished on the golf course or what indiscretions are spilled over a few martinis at the 19th hole."

"Or behind closed doors? I've never seen you like this, Rocco."

"Like what?"

"Angry. It's out of character. What's eating you?"

Rocco leaned back in his chair, slowly counting the cracks in the ceiling. His anger choked him like a tight collar. Adrian was right that it wasn't like him. So, what exactly was bothering him?

"Didn't it go well last night with Detective Reardon?" she asked.

"No, that's not it," he said, trying to pinpoint what was gnawing at him. Things with Maggie were heading in the right direction, albeit at a snail's pace.

"Well?"

"I think it's Barbara. Aside from her love for you, I thought I was her best friend."

"You are. And mine too."

"Then why didn't she confide in me? I had her in my house for days after the murder and she never said a word."

"Rocco, it's because you are her friend that she didn't tell you."

"I don't get it."

"She didn't want to put you in that position."

"I still don't get it."

"She didn't want you to have to make the choice between being a loyal friend or doing the right thing. And she didn't tell me because she thought she was protecting me."

"Barbara shouldn't have carried that burden alone."

"She thought she was doing the right thing. It's done. And now you say we have to play dirty and I don't know how."

"The rules have changed. Macy Friedman is going to see Barbara this morning. Then he's going to have a one on one with the City Attorney. Everybody owes somebody and I'll bet he's no exception."

"I've always hated politics, but I'm starting warm. Is that contradictory? Hating something unless it's working to my own advantage?"

"Human nature."

The tears were starting to well in Adrian's eyes again.

"Stop crying and wipe the fairy dust from your eyes. It's out of our hands. You need to be strong and work on what we can control. And we're in control of saving the gallery."

"I'll try. I promise."

"I'm sorry for being so rough on you, Adrian. I've been taking it out on you, but the gallery's survival is up to the two of us. At least for now. It's the one thing we can still do for Barbara."

"I just want her home where she belongs, the sooner the better."

"It'll take as long as it takes."

"But I called the jail this morning and they won't even let me visit her."

"Patience." He looked around at the gallery walls, still filled with artwork from the last show. Calypso's wild, colorful collages filled one wall and Paloma Blanca's jewelry sat safely behind glass. Mary Rose's traditional landscapes hung in contrast to the washed-out white on white abstracts by Misty Waters. Rocco's own metal sculptures stood like naughty Easter Island sentinels waiting for him to carry them home. Belinda Blume's Gaia sculpture was absent. The beautiful goddess was nothing but broken shards covered in blood. What remained of it sat in the evidence room at the police department. The gallery felt empty and abandoned. A place of joy and beauty and refuge was now sullied by the reality of death.

He needed to bring it back to life. Saving The Mosaic Gallery was as important as saving Barbara. They were one and the same.

"We need to focus. Start calling the artist's to pick up their work."

"The show certainly came to an abrupt end. A dead body can do that," she smiled and it felt good. There wasn't much to smile about except getting in this one last dig at the man who'd shared her lover. "That was wicked of me, I know, but I don't miss Armando one bit."

"Nor do I," he admitted as he pushed the address book across the desk. "We need to prepare for a new show before we become another failed gallery. Make some calls and we'll get the group together. They need to pick up their art and we need to fill them in and discuss the future. We'll see how things play out and proceed from there. I'll be damned if Armando's ghost will pull this place into the grave with him."

"Barbara may have signed off on the deed, but I don't feel like The Mosaic is ours."

"As soon as this mess is resolved, we'll sign it right back to her."

Adrian agreed, opened the address book and picked up the phone.

"Okay, let's get to work," she said.

Rocco got up and walked to her side of the desk, took the receiver from her hand and sat it back into its cradle. He grasped her hands and lifted her from her chair. She rose with a grunt.

"There's one thing we need to do first," Rocco said.

He walked her through the front door and across the side yard and the two of them sat on the bench under the shade of the gnarled mesquite tree. The warm air hung onto the humidity from last night's rain as a few stray clouds streaked across the brilliant aquamarine sky.

"We need to clear our negativity," he said.

They closed their eyes, inhaled deeply, and held their palms upward.

All was silent but for the garbled chatter of a quail family as they trotted single file across the yard and into the brush and the occasional mesquite leaf that softly whispered as it fluttered to the damp ground.

* * * *

As was her usual routine, Maggie Reardon stopped at the mini-mart on her way to headquarters. More important than stocking up on quick snacks were her daily visits with Carlos. He'd been behind the counter since she was a child and he always greeted her with a wide smile and a kind word. She noticed that he'd picked up the habit, consciously or otherwise, of covering his mouth when he smiled, hiding the teeth that were only a few shades lighter than his leathered Mexican skin. In his broken English, he had praised the school work she'd shared with him when she came in for candy after school. He gave her non-judgmental advice through her rebellious teens. He was prouder still as she blossomed into a strong, young woman. He treated her like a daughter and was happy to fill the role of surrogate father when disaster struck. He helped fill the void when her parents were killed on the highway and helped the devastated girl through the worst of times.

And he shared her joys in the best of times.

She loved him like family.

After leaving headquarters Maggie drove through the west end of town, up one street and down another, keeping an eye out for trouble in what was unfolding as a trouble free day. The monsoon had let up and the sun was shining. Her time with Rocco the night before had gone okay. Better than expected. The door remained open despite everything and she was feeling good about the prospect of their growing closer. It was looking like this was one chance she was taking where the odds were stacking up in her favor.

About damn time, she thought as she turned the corner.

The dispatchers voice cracked through the radio static, disturbing her reverie.

"ASDM," the voice said. A body had been discovered at the Arizona Sonoran Desert Museum. So much for a trouble-free day. Ambulance and personnel were on the way and Detective Maggie Reardon pulled a u-turn and headed farther west. She turned up Speedway and crossed Silverbell as she headed up the hill. Rocco. All she could hope for was that it wasn't Rocco. He donated his time as a docent at the museum. Was this one of his days? He was always filling in on his off days for another docent who couldn't make it, so he could be there at any time. She hit the gas and turned on the siren as she wound around the curves, climbing higher up the foothills toward the museum.

Speedway morphed into Gates Pass as she sped through mountains dotted with aged saguaros. They stood tall and silent, witnesses to the passage of time. Going down hill, the Old Tucson Studios stood in the desert valley below, surrounded by cotton farms and the Tohono O'odham Indian Reservation. Kitt Peak towered in the distance. She could hear the pop, pop of gunfire from the shooting range as she hung a right onto Kinney Road. She'd driven at warp speed, cutting a twenty minute drive down to fifteen, all the time thinking of Rocco and what she'd do if she'd already lost him. The museum loomed on her left and she sped past the ironwood trees and down the narrow road that led to the parking lot, turned in, slammed on her brakes and exited the car. Maggie ran past the United States, Arizona and Mexican flags that fluttered overhead. She crossed the front patio area where javelina sculptures stood under the green palo verde tree, and approached the ticket window.

"I'm sorry," the woman said. "But we've had to close unexpectedly."

Maggie caught her breath, then pulled out her badge and flashed it.

"It would've been easier if you'd come through the back," the woman said.

"How do I get there from here?"

"Let me call Gene," she said. "My God, this is a public relations disaster. Some guy managed to fall into the javelina enclosure. How stupid is that?"

Maggie grunted.

She paced, waiting for Gene, whoever he was and wondering why he was necessary.

A middle-aged man pulled up in a golf cart and waved her in his direction. He wore a Tilly hat and tan Dockers and his white shirt had an ASDM emblem sewn onto the sleeve.

"Hop in," he said. "I can get you there faster. It's quite a walk from here."

She slid in beside him.

"Why didn't you drive up through the back?"

"I didn't know there was a back," she said. "I've only been here once and came through the front." More memories of Rocco surfaced. How confident he'd been talking to the crowd that day. She'd found herself attracted to him, despite the large snake he held in his rough hands. The look he'd given her said he felt the same.

"I'll get you there quick, officer." Gene said, speeding up the cart.

"Detective," she corrected. "Was it an employee?"

"Nobody we recognized is all I know. How the hell he managed to fall off that bridge is beyond me. Must've been one clumsy fellow."

Maggie was relieved. Rocco was safe. Now she could concentrate on the business at hand. Let the cop take over and get the job done. Logic over emotion, just how she liked it. One less complication. She was heading into her comfort zone. A dead body was easier to deal with than a live person any day.

＊ ＊ ＊ ＊

Things were in full swing and yellow crime scene tape was already laced around a large area.

Gene stopped the cart. "It looks like this is as far as I can go," he said.

"I appreciate it."

"This is the most excitement we've had around here since 1987."

"87?"

"It was all over the news."

"My memory doesn't go back that far. What happened?"

"Two big horn sheep were killed. Bloody nightmare of a mess. Some bastard severed the head and a leg of our six year old ram. You guys never did solve it," he continued. "They guessed it was some satanic ritual, but I think it was some sicko getting his kicks."

"They should've tried harder, but animal abuse doesn't get the attention it should. That's bad enough, but nine times out of ten it's just practice."

"How's that?"

"They graduate to people. Damn near every serial killer out there cuts his teeth on animals. It'd be nice to put 'em all away before their taste for blood escalates. It's horrible."

"Evil always is," he said. "How can you deal with that stuff?"

"Somebody has to."

"You must have a strong stomach."

The yellow crime scene tape stopped Gene in his tracks.

"I guess this is as far as I can take you," he said. "It's a short walk. Just follow the path down."

"Thanks again, Gene. You've been a big help."

Mid-morning was heating up in more ways than one. She wiped the perspiration from her brow with her shirt sleeve as she walked, glad it was a downhill path. The brittle bushes bloomed with cheerful yellow flowers and the air smelled fresh from yesterday's rain. It would have been a perfect morning if there wasn't some dead guy in the mix. She could see the police and emergency vehicles below. She paused to catch her breath, then headed down the path that lead to the bridge.

Just one more day in paradise.

CHAPTER FOUR

The Corpse

Jerry Montana was the first officer to approach when Detective Maggie Reardon reached the scene. She and Jerry had formed an uneasy truce, but it took a lot of work and their attempts were mediocre at best. His young trainee, Aaron Iverson, followed puppy-like behind him, his pale mid-western complexion rising to a brilliant pink. It might have been caused by the Tucson heat. Or the shock of confronting his first dead body. At least he wasn't throwing up in the bushes, a response she'd seen more times than she cared to remember. She'd damn near lost it herself the first time, but being a woman she wouldn't give the other cops the satisfaction. They'd fought her at every turn, so she'd just swallowed hard and gotten down to business. The boys club would never know that first body gave her nightmares for weeks.

Being a cop was tough. Being a woman cop was tougher. Like they say, Fred Astaire could dance, but Ginger Rogers did all the steps backwards and in high heels. A woman was expected to prove herself ten times more than if she were a man. And for half the recognition. But the captain was supportive and that's what mattered, so she learned to suck it up. And they learned she could dish it out in equal portions, if not worse.

She got even by making detective in record time.

And they learned when to back off.

"You're still pretty bruised up," Jerry said with a smirk. "But that shiner's starting to fade."

"Thanks again, both of you, for showing up when you did," she said. She'd have liked smacking the smirk off his face and giving him a clever come-back, but she bit her tongue. After all, they had shown up and crashed through her door right when Marty the ex was about to get the best of her.

She unconsciously lifted her hand to her swollen lip.

Keeping her mouth shut was never easy. Back in school she pulled down A's and B's, but there was always a teacher who scrawled "Margaret must learn self-control" across the bottom of her report card. One semester five teachers all wrote the exact same thing. She was sure they put their heads together in the teacher's lounge and wrote it in unison just to tick her off. Her occasional outbursts and disruptions were beside the point. Her father blamed the hot-headed Reardon genes and let it go at that. Her mother said that the qualities that drove everybody nuts were the qualities that would give her the strength to take on an adult world. They were both right.

She never liked being called Margaret. She was a Maggie through and through. Margaret was some sissy girl who wore ruffles and little velvet bows and never had skinned knees. Or she was Sister Mary Margaret, shrouded in black, holding a ruler to protect her from the world when she wasn't using it to rap across some kid's knuckles until they bled. Even her mother came to realize that Margaret was a poor fit and they started calling her Maggie before she graduated from diapers.

Maggie looked at Aaron. The Arizona sun was losing its battle to toughen his skin, poor guy. His complexion slowly drained from carnation pink back to his usual Minnesota pallor. There are some things a person gets used to, but the sight of a lifeless body wasn't one of them. When the cops found them they weren't made up with rosy cheeks and a peaceful smile glued on by some funeral parlor. More often than not, they were bruised and bloody and surrounded by an aura of violence. It was never pretty, but you learned to deal with it.

It was part of the job.

"It just looks like some freakin' accident," said Jerry.

"A freak accident," Aaron echoed.

"Dumb guy just fell over the rail. End of story," said Jerry.

Maggie looked over the railing to the body below. An employee was herding the last of the javelinas into their enclosure, clearing the area so that the police could safely enter.

"We'll know more when we get down there," she said.

The body was crumpled under a patch of cacti. Most of it anyway. The attendant kicked the last straggler from where it stood nibbling at an unattached arm that lay in the dirt. When the last of the beasts entered the enclosure the man snapped the gate shut and yelled up to them.

"All's clear."

Jerry started to head down and she stopped him.

"Who found him?"

He pointed to a couple with a young boy standing several feet away. "I want to speak with them first."

"I already did," said Jerry.

"A couple more minutes won't kill you," she said, heading over to where they stood.

The young boy wandered off, entranced by the police cars and emergency vehicles. Maggie approached the parents. Their wardrobes screamed *tourist*. The woman's polyester and two inch heels fought the rising temperature. The man wore inappropriate shoes for a desert hike. She asked them to repeat their story.

"We just want to get out of here," said the husband.

"This'll just take a few minutes," said Maggie as she took out her pen and flipped open her notepad.

"Horrible, just horrible," said the wife, looking over at her son. "Something like this could scar a child for life."

"He didn't understand, honey," the husband reassured her.

"Would you tell me how you found the body?" asked Maggie.

"Let me do the talking," he said. "You're too upset. We thought this would be a nice place to bring Jimmy, to show him about nature. We want him to be aware of the world around him, you know?"

"Not this kind of world," his wife mumbled. Her tears fell in a river of dark mascara from her painted eyes.

"Go on," Maggie said.

"Jimmy saw those statues out front and wanted to see the real live pigs, so we headed this way."

"He was so excited," said the wife.

"Jimmy was running a good ten feet ahead of us and we were playing catch up when he reached the bridge."

"I took out my camera," the wife said. "I wanted to take his picture as he was looking down from the bridge. He's so darn cute, we just can't get enough pictures of him. They grow up so fast. It's sad, really."

"Anyway," the husband interrupted, "Jimmy looked down and yelled back at me. He asked me why they feed the pigs clothes."

Maggie resisted the urge to correct them. Javelina's weren't pigs. They were peccaries. But what would be the point? It hardly mattered considering the circumstances.

"Oh, God," the wife moaned. "He thought they'd fed the pigs clothes." The wife held both hands over her mouth, her body trembling.

"We caught up with him and looked down. The pigs were clustered in one spot and it looked like they were chewing on some cloth."

"Jimmy was right. They were eating a shirt of all things," said the wife.

"Yea, it looked like somebody's shirt sleeve."

"And then we, we..." the wife began.

"And then we saw that there was an arm in it."

"I grabbed Jimmy's hand," said the wife, "And I led him away as fast as I could, all the while him telling me he wanted to keep watching the pigs. I told him it was impolite to watch them while they were eating. Stupid, but I didn't know what else to say."

"That was quick thinking," said Maggie. "You did just fine."

"We didn't know what to do," said the husband. "I was kicking myself for leaving my cell phone in the car. I just wanted to call somebody and scream for help."

"I spotted the emergency phone," said the wife, pointing in the direction of some dead saguaros. "So we went over and picked it up and reported what we saw. Can we go now?"

"Just a few more questions."

"We already told the other officer everything we know," he said. "We just want to get Jimmy out of here."

Maggie looked over to where little Jimmy was standing, a typical boy easily entertained by the cluster of squad cars and emergency vehicles and flashing lights. He was overdressed, as though his mother had encased him safely into a cocoon. She turned back to face his parents.

"Did you see any other people? When you were walking towards the enclosure did you notice anyone passing in the other direction?"

"Have you ever tried to keep up with a rambunctious five year old?" asked the husband. "It's like trying to herd cats. We weren't paying attention to anything but Jimmy. He can be a handful, I tell you. We've got to watch him every second or he's gone in a flash."

"He can be playing in the yard one minute and the second you look away he's gone. It's enough to give me a heart attack."

"So you noticed no one?" Maggie asked, trying to draw the woman's focus from her obsession with her only child. No matter how hard one tries to protect them, the reality of life has a way of sneaking in. She hoped the father was right, that Jimmy was oblivious to what he'd witnessed. At least that would buy him one more innocent day.

"I think a few people passed us," said the wife, trying her best to be helpful as she pulled at the dress that clung to her legs. "But I couldn't tell you if they were men or women or the abominable snowman. It wasn't our focus." She kept shifting her weight from one aching foot to the other, pulling at the perspiration soaked fabric and glancing in the direction of her boy.

They'd had enough discomfort for one morning and she wasn't getting any information that could be useful, so Maggie thanked them for their time. She wrote down their contact information and flagged over one of the officers.

"You've been helpful," she lied to the man as his wife walked away to retrieve their son. "If I have more questions I'll contact you."

"I hope this isn't going to interfere with our plans. We're on a tight itinerary and head out in four days for the Grand Canyon, then home. I've got to get back to work on time, you know? Jobs don't grow on trees."

Maggie handed him her card. "I hope the rest of your trip is more pleasant. If you haven't heard back from me, please give me a call before you go, in case I need to speak with you again."

"I don't know what we could add to what we've already told you. And that other guy," he said, pointing in Jerry Montana's direction. She could tell by the way he said *that other guy* that Jerry had left his usual impression. He wasn't the poster boy for public relations.

When the officer approached she asked him to escort the family to the front gate, then returned to the bridge where Jerry Montana and Aaron Iverson stood. Jerry held a camera and was taking distance photos of the scene below.

"It looks like those doggies found themselves one hell of a new chew toy," said Jerry.

The man who had herded the javelinas led them down the slope.

"I never realized that javelinas are carnivores," Maggie said. "And I'm a Tucsonan."

"Not as a rule," he replied, "but they're creatures of opportunity. Did you know they can gobble down prickly pear cactus spines and all?"

"I know they're tougher than rawhide, but they don't usually attack people."

"Not usually. But when they wander through neighborhoods sometimes a snow bird or newcomer feeds them. Problem is, if they get used to it and someone comes along who doesn't give them something, they get pissed as grizzlies and attack. And it ain't pretty."

"But this group is enclosed and well fed."

He looked down to where the body lay crumpled in the enclosure.

"They're omnivores. Like I said, they're creatures of opportunity. And it looks like opportunity fell right into their laps."

"Omnivore," Jerry mumbled, "sounds like some kinda car."

Maggie watched as the javelina herder climbed up the slope and out of sight.

Maggie, Jerry and Aaron descended and stood over the flannel wrapped arm. Jerry took

more photos as Maggie walked over to the cluster of cacti. The rest of the body lay in a semi-fetal

position, as if the corpse was just sleeping peacefully in cactus. On first observation, he appeared to have no wounds other than some abrasions from falling down the slope and the chew marks from the enthusiastic javelinas on his exposed flesh. But there were no head wounds. No bullet holes. No knife in his back. Maybe Jerry Montana was right. It could have been a freak accident.

But Maggie was never one to accept first impressions.

She'd wait for the coroner's report before she wrote this one off. Something wasn't computing. Something gnawed at her, that gut instinct that rarely failed. Autopsy and physical evidence put the icing on the cake, but it was a cop's instinct that led it all in the right direction. And it was the cop who connected the puzzle pieces.

Maggie motioned to Montana and Iverson.

"Let's get photos of the rest of this poor guy," she said. Montana's camera clicked away, capturing the body from every angle as Maggie and Aaron measured the distance from the bridge above to where the body lay in repose.

"Get over here Iverson," said Montana. "Help me turn this guy over."

As the color drained from the rookie's face, she wondered how anybody could turn so white. He was whiter than new fallen snow, as if a bottle of bleach had been poured over him. But he walked over and helped turn over the body, doing his best to suppress his gag reflex. His sensitivity glowed in contrast to Jerry Montana's callousness.

The quiet town he'd come from hadn't afforded him much practice in hard crime, but the kid might make a good cop after all.

* * * *

The camera sounded its final clicks, then Montana told the attendants in his usual, crude manner that they could clear the scene and put the guy in the meat wagon. He had no respect for the living or the dead. Maggie slipped on her rubber gloves, knelt over the body and felt his pockets. All they held were a half-empty pack of smokes and a disposable lighter. No wallet, no credit cards, no family photos, nothing. Strange. An unfortunate tourist? Someone just passing through? Someone with something to hide?

"This is a real fresh one," said Jerry, giving the corpse a nudge with his foot. "Still looks like an accident to me. Ripping off that arm was enough to kill him."

"Uh-huh," said Aaron.

Something tickled at Maggie's brain.

"C'mon over here," she said, motioning Aaron to the body. "What do you see?"

Aaron studied the still form and shrugged. Then he saw it too.

"There's no exsanguination!"

"Do you know what that indicates?"

"Sure," he said. "He was dead before he landed. Otherwise he'd have bled out."

"That puts a different slant on things, doesn't it?"

Aaron nodded.

"He could've had a heart attack," said Jerry in defense of his initial opinion.

"It's a possibility," said Maggie, "but I want every trash bin on the grounds gone through."

"Why?" groaned Montana, not looking forward to what he considered a menial task.

"If it wasn't an accident, it's sure as hell easier looking for evidence here than sifting through mountains of trash once it hits the dump, don't you think?"

"Don't want to get your own hands dirty?"

"I don't have to."

The three of them climbed back up to the bridge, and she walked the length of the railings, then back again. She leaned forward as far as she could from every angle. Once again, something didn't compute.

"Come over here, you two," she said. "Montana, lean over the railing as far as you can."

"What for?"

"Do you have to question everything? Because you're taller."

Jerry leaned over the railing.

"Now you," she said to Aaron.

The results were the same.

Maggie pulled the tape measure from her pocket and handed it to Aaron, then pulled out her notepad.

"I need you two to measure the height, here and over there."

They called out the measurements and she wrote them down.

"That ought to do it." She flipped her notepad closed and shoved it into her pocket. She ran her fingers through her short red hair, damp with perspiration. The day was warm and the sky was clear overhead, but roasted marshmallow clouds had begun to gather beyond the distant mountains, dark and threatening.

"What are you up to?" asked Jerry.

"You didn't lose your balance."

"So?"

"That ought to tell you something."

Jerry stood there looking stupid, while Aaron looked like a big, shiny lightbulb just went off in his head. He was a rookie, but he was definitely smarter than the cop who was showing him the ropes.

Maggie gave him a wink as they headed off in opposite directions.

CHAPTER FIVE

Dancing with Devils

The woman peered through the motel room curtain and smiled. She unlocked the window and slid it open. She wasn't supposed to unlock it but she always did, just long enough to air out the smell of his stale cigarette smoke. The sun shone on the cars in the parking lot and the only remnants of rain were the puddles collected in the blacktop's depressions. The previous afternoon she had turned off the tv a good hour before her husband's expected return. There were times she'd seen him touch the top of the set when he walked in, like he was testing to see if it was warm. He wouldn't understand that its noise made her feel less lonely. Or why she had disobeyed him. For the most part she watched cartoons. She couldn't say why, but they comforted her like old friends. She knew that wasn't right, that he was the only friend she needed. He'd told her so and that should have been enough. But she watched her animated friends just the same.

She knew it was nothing but a bit of crazy somewhere inside her head, but sometimes she thought the characters whispered to her. As if they were trying to remind her of something from long ago, but it was a memory that refused to come to the surface no matter how hard she tried. He had come back last evening with his pockets full and a satisfied grin on his face. They'd gone out walking as he'd promised. They didn't go far, just up and down the street, but it felt good to smell some fresh air beyond the oppressiveness of the small room. It was nice to see a face other than her own reflection in the mirror.

Some of the people they passed on the sidewalk saddened her. Scantily dressed women flirted with men who drove slowly past, some stopping to talk to them. And sometimes a man opened his car door so a woman could slide into the passenger seat next to him. And there were panhandlers begging for change, mostly addicts and drinkers desperate for their next fix or their next bottle. Shadows spilled below the street lights like dark and ominous ghosts. They scared her, but it was better than being cooped up in their motel room. She loved the freedom of their walks. She smiled as a group of teens passed them, barely younger than herself. They wore baggy pants slung below their behinds and chips on their shoulders and spoke in a language foreign to her. She was fascinated by their strange body piercings and tattooes and the odd gestures they made with their hands.

"Don't look at them," her husband said. "They're Satan's children."

She lowered her head so as not to make eye contact, glad he was there to protect her even if she was grown up. He told her the world was a minefield and maneuvered her safely down the sidewalk and into a small café and over to a table far from the entrance.

They'd stopped for a special treat, burritos eaten at a real table instead of their usual meal sitting on the lumpy motel mattress sharing a bag of take-out. She'd been afraid of her first bite, convinced that Mexican food wasn't meant to be eaten by anyone who wasn't born to it. But it was good, unlike what she'd tasted in New Mexico. That food had burned like a branding iron on her taste buds and made her eyes water.

Except for the occasional glance over his shoulder, he seemed more relaxed than he'd been lately. It made her nervous when he was antsy. She could never make sense of it and his edginess rubbed off on her like a contagion and grew into a gigantic knot in her stomach.

After eating they walked to a small market and stocked up on odds and ends. He'd even let her pick out something. She'd chosen a box of cereal she'd seen advertised on the television. It had a colorful cartoon character on the front of the package who was smiling at her, surrounded by a rainbow of puffy, sugared grains.

They'd stopped in the motel office on their way back. Her husband had pulled out some wrinkled bills and paid for a week in advance. She hoped that meant he was thinking of staying, of finally settling down in one place.

The possibility lifted her spirits but she hesitated to ask, afraid his answer might break the spell.

When they returned to their room he made love to her.

And this morning he'd left early in search of another day's work.

Things were looking up.

She slid the window shut, locked it and closed the curtains, then walked over to the dresser and grabbed the box of cereal. She tore it open and reached her hand inside. Little puffs of primary colors fell to the floor as she shoved a handful into her mouth. Holding the box, she plopped down onto the bed and reached for the remote.

* * * *

At The Mosaic Gallery the afternoon sun spilled across the room. Rocco La Crosse scowled at the blood stains on the wooden floor. The planks were dark where Armando's body had lain, an outline of violence that refused to go away. Despite repeated scrubbings the tell-tale shadow remained, as if Armando Salazar's ghost refused to leave.

"It's useless," said Adrian Velikson. "You might as well give up."

Rocco rose to his feet and tossed the soggy rag through the air, where it landed dead-center into the waste basket.

"Good shot," said Adrian, "You should've been a basketball player."

"At my height? I'm about belly high to those guys and five times wider." He looked around the room. "Give me a hand here. Let's move these shelves to the other wall."

Adrian looked over at the empty shelf unit where Armando had displayed the Mexican artifact rip-offs that were the cause of all their troubles. If he hadn't been smuggling cocaine in them, if Barbara hadn't found out, if he hadn't attacked her, then she wouldn't be in jail waiting for a murder charge. So many ifs. The bastard was as much trouble dead as he'd been alive. He'd been Barbara Atwell's blind spot, but being charged for his murder was overkill for not seeing through his charming demeanor and slick bullshit.

Adrian missed her partner and prayed Rocco could somehow, someway work his magic.

The tall shelf was more awkward than heavy, so after taking down some paintings to clear up wall space the two of them walked it across the room. The blood stain stood out like a guy in jeans at a black tie affair. "Let's put the folding table right over it," he said. "A little more rearranging and it'll never show."

Adrian puffed from the effort as they dragged the table over, unfolded the legs, and placed it over the death stain.

"Appropriate," she said. "The table where the Latin lover poured the bubbly and served snacks and hit on damn near every female in the room. Next reception he can look up and see how unnecessary he really was."

"Learn to let go," he said, but his words were shallow. "It's unhealthy and resolves nothing." But he couldn't disagree with a word she'd said.

Macy Friedman, the attorney he had on it, would do what he could. It was out of their hands and worrying would do nothing to change the outcome. But he worried too.

"It'll be okay," he reassured her.

"Do you have a crystal ball?"

There was a loud banging on the front door. Adrian glanced down at her watch.

"The meeting isn't until five," she said. "It's barely three."

Rocco walked to the door, unlocked and opened it. Belinda Blume stood there, frizzy brown hair dancing chaotically around her scowling face.

"Belinda? You're early, but you know you're always welcome. Come on in."

She shoved past him and stomped into the room.

"Can the niceties," she said. "Where's Adrian?"

Before he could answer, she had entered the second room and stood there, arms crossed and tapping her foot like a stubborn kid.

"Hello Belinda."

She uncrossed her arms and held out her hand, opening and closing it impatiently.

"My check. I'm here for my money."

Adrian walked over to the desk and sifted through the pile of checks she'd written. "Will you have something for the next show?" she asked, trying to hold her patience.

"You're kidding me, right?"

Rocco joined them. It sounded like Adrian was in need of a buffer.

"Nice to see you," he said.

"Cut the crap, Rocco." Then to Adrian: "Do you two really think I'd want to show here again? To be associated with a gallery where there's been a murder? My Gaia is gone, thanks to Barbara. My works deserve more respect than that and so do I. I've made arrangements with a more *upscale* gallery where I can triple my prices."

"And reduce your chances of selling anything at all," Adrian said. "And thanks so much for your concern over Barbara."

"Just give me my check and I'm out of here."

Adrian rose from the desk and handed Belinda her check.

"For your Gaia. As promised."

Belinda looked down at the amount scrawled on the check.

"This isn't right," she said. "The price I had on it was higher."

"Minus our commission."

"It's your fault it was stolen."

Rocco interrupted and filled her in on her precious Gaia's demise and the role it played in Armando's murder. Belinda was unconcerned that Barbara was in jail.

"That's even worse," she said. "My masterpiece wasn't stolen, it was destroyed. I should have it's full value. Or more."

"On what planet?"

"You've got what you came for," said Rocco, taking her by the arm. "I suggest you go now."

"I deserve more."

"It's not going to happen," he said as he led her to the door. Then very formally and totally lacking in sincerity, he added, "I wish you success in your new endeavor."

"You're nothing but crooks," she said, shoving the check into her purse. "And murderers. Do you really think for a minute this place is going to survive? You're going to crash and burn." Rocco slammed the door behind her before she could spew any more venom.

"Is she gone?"

"She's gone."

Adrian was crying again.

"Don't cry," he said as he re-entered the room. "People might catch on that under your tough exterior you're mush. I think we should be rejoicing, don't you?"

"What if she's right? What if we're doomed to failure?"

"I won't let that happen and neither will you. We've just eliminated an artist who's always been a thorn in our sides, so I'd say things are looking up."

The phone rang. Adrian took a deep breath before picking up.

"The Mosaic Gallery," she said. "Yes, he's right here. Hold on a sec."

"It's one of the docents," she said and handed him the phone.

"This is Rocco."

He held it to his ear and listened.

"You're kidding me, who was it?"

The voice on the other end droned on.

"Thanks for letting me know," he said and handed the receiver back to Adrian. She replaced it onto its cradle.

"Now what?"

"They found a dead body out at the Desert Museum."

* * * *

That afternoon Detective Maggie Reardon sat at her desk at head-quarters. She focused on the computer screen and punched in the numbers she had scrawled on her notepad at the crime scene. Her gut told her that it was, indeed, a crime scene and not some freak accident like Jerry Montana had assumed. And she was determined to prove it. First glances can prove deceptive and snap assumptions misleading. Any cop with experience should know that, especially someone who'd been around as long as Jerry. No wonder he was always passed up for promotions. If the pay wasn't so lousy and they didn't need every cop they could get, she was ure they'd have washed him out ages ago.

She picked up the phone and punched in an extension.

"Maggie Reardon here," she said. "I was wondering if you've started on that John Doe from the Desert Museum yet. No? Could you do me a favor?"

"For you, Maggie? No problem" said the woman at the other end.

"I'm trying to figure something out here and need to know his height."

"Hold on, okay?"

Maggie shuffled through her morning's notes as she waited. She'd make sure the crime scene tape stayed up until she proved her suspicions, just in case they'd missed something and needed to go over the scene again. With their pr already in damage control mode, the Museum was sure to give her an earful about having to stay closed. Murder was inconvenient. Especially for the victim.

She stared at the computer screen, waiting for the last set of numbers.

"Maggie?"

"I'm still here." She jotted down the man's height. "Thanks," she said, hung up the phone and punched the information onto the keyboard.

The animated figure, the bridge and the railings appeared on the screen and Maggie started playing with the numbers. Height of railing, height of John Doe, distance from the bridge to where the body landed. No matter where she placed him on the bridge the results were the same.

It was just as she suspected.

The calculations proved that there was no way Mr. John Doe could have gone over that railing without assistance. The architects and engineers would certainly have designed the bridge to avoid just such an accident. They had done their job and now she had to do hers. So who was he? And who had hoisted him over the railing and into the javelina enclosure? They'd already determined that he was dead before he land-ed, but there were no apparent attack wounds on his body other than those from the javelinas. So how was he killed? The autopsy should provide some answers. Although it was the crime that mattered not the motive, motive helped in zeroing in on the perpetrator. And identifying the victim was an important step toward some answers.

But he was a nameless mystery.

She called the extension again.

"Just a head's up," she said. "Our John Doe was definitely a mur-der."

Maggie hung up and rose from her desk.

She needed to think and she needed a smoke.

She reached for her purse and the phone rang.

"Detective Reardon," she said.

"Maggie, this is Rocco."

Her heart did its usual dance at the sound of his voice.

"Hello Rocco."

"I got a call from the Museum. A bunch of gossip really, but they're closed and my volunteer days have been cancelled until further notice. What's going on?"

"A dead body."

Blunt, to the point, no details.

"At the javelina enclosure, I know, but I hoped you could fill me in."

"There's nothing to add yet. And Rocco, you know I can't discuss an ongoing investigation."

"Ever the professional. I should've known better."

"Don't apologize."

"Should I get used to bodies sprouting up wherever I turn?"

"Get close enough to me and it's bound to happen."

He changed the subject. "About last night…"

Maggie stiffened, waiting for the usual *I'm dumping you* excuse. She'd heard it more times than she cared to count.

"Go ahead."

"I was wondering when I could see you again."

An inaudible sigh of relief as she jumped on it like a cat on catnip. "How about tonight?"

"I was hoping that would be your answer."

"My house is a mess. Can we make it your place?"

"Seven-ish?"

"That works for me."

"I'll be waiting."

Maggie hung up, grabbed her purse and headed through the front door.

Leaning against the building she inhaled deeply. Nothing like a little nicotine mixed with fresh air to calm her down and help her think.

Jerry Montana and Aaron Iverson walked across the parking lot in her direction. She'd try not to gloat too much when she told Jerry what she'd discovered. She loved being right as much as he hated being wrong. Were it not for their truce, she'd have found great pleasure in rubbing it in until his skin burned.

"You guys finished combing through the trash bins?"

"No way," answered Aaron in his Minnesotan accent. "We're about half way is all, but we'll finish it up tomorrow, you betcha."

"Too bad you couldn't join us," said Jerry. "But you wouldn't want to get those pretty little hands dirty."

"You gotta love the pecking order, right Jerry?"

"I don't know about him but I'm ready for a hot shower and some peppermint schnapps," said Aaron.

"You were good out there today."

"Thanks."

When they reached the front entrance she said, "Oh Jerry, just thought you'd like to know something."

"Depends," he said, turning to face her.

"It was no accident."

CHAPTER SIX

Politics and Paint Brushes

"Be patient," Rocco La Crosse said to Adrian as the artists trickled one by one into the gallery. "We're bound to lose a few more, just like we lost Belinda. People come into our lives and people move on."

"What if there aren't enough of them left to put on a show? Then what?"

"Those that support us will continue to do so. Those that don't are no loss. This is a time of change and we need to move forward. If worse comes to worse we can all clear out the backlog in our studios to fill the walls. Hell, I've got enough at home for a one man show. Maybe two."

Adrian rose from where she sat behind the desk and reached for her pile of papers.

"I'd be more comfortable if you did the talking," she said.

The metal folding chairs in the first gallery room began to fill. The space was thick with inaudible whispers that turned silent when Rocco entered. Adrian sat down and fidgeted with her papers, avoiding eye contact.

Rocco stood before the seated artists.

"This is a difficult time," he began. "First I'd like to thank you for coming on such short notice."

"Where's Barbara?" asked Calypso. Orange Bozo the Clown hair clashed with her magenta blouse like melted crayons run amok. Her hair danced in crazy strands, as though she'd just dragged herself out of bed and was struggling to get her bearings. "I haven't heard anything since, well, since…" Her voice drifted off as her attention span took its usual decline. Her focus turned to her bright purple skirt, fingers tracing the stitches along the borders of the multi-colored floral appliques.

Rocco was direct.

"For those of you who haven't heard, Barbara has confessed to killing Armando."

Gasps of disbelief echoed through the room.

"I don't understand," said a bewildered Mary Rose. The elderly woman shook her head. "I thought it was a robbery."

"She probably had good reason," said Paloma Blanca. "He never was a prize."

"I'll be brief," said Rocco. "Barbara's in jail. At this point she hasn't been charged, but we should have an answer soon and I'll keep you posted. Bottom line is we're hoping they see it as self-defense." He filled them in about Armando's cocaine smuggling and how it was accomplished. And how he'd attacked Barbara when she found him out.

"And she hit him with the Gaia statue? How utterly ironic." Paloma Blanca smirked, looked around the room and stretched her neck to see who was seated behind her. "And where is the great Belinda? I'd have thought she'd be here."

"She came and left," said Rocco. "She's decided to go to another gallery. If any of you are uncomfortable and want to follow suit we understand and there will be no ill feelings. You can pick up your art and your money and leave. If you choose to stay, Adrian and I will be in charge until things settle down. I needn't say that your support will be more than appreciated."

Only Paloma Blanca rose. Dark eyes peered through her long black hair as she scanned the room. She walked over to the display case that held her jewelry and began placing the pieces into her large tote bag.

"I'll make arrangements elsewhere," she said.

"I can't understand why you won't be staying," said Mary Rose. "You've been here so long. You're family my dear."

"*Mi familia?* It's run it's course so consider this our divorce. I'm cutting ties and moving on." She walked over to Adrian and reached for her check. "Well, it looks like you've got Barbara all to yourself again, just like you wanted."

Adrian mumbled an expletive under her breath.

Paloma ignored the group as she headed for the exit.

The door slammed behind her.

"Not even a 'nice to have known you'," said Mary Rose. "I'm truly shocked at her behavior."

"Didn't you know she was banging Armando? That's probably why she stayed as long as she did." Calypso's turquoise and silver bracelet jangled as she rearranged her gaudy gypsy skirt.

"Common knowledge my dear, but hardly an excuse for her rudeness."

"I never could figure what he saw in her," said Calypso, her jealousy showing at being one of the few he'd rejected.

"She was female and she liked to play," said Adrian. "That was enough."

The words stung. Calypso liked to play, but despite her blatant efforts he'd never given her a tumble.

"Two prima donnas gone," she said. "And one Lothario." She stretched her hands dramatically upward, waving them to and fro. "A blessing from the Goddess."

"Let's not deteriorate into gossip," said Mary Rose. "It serves no purpose nor should one speak ill of the dead. It's bad karma."

The watercolor artist, Misty Waters, spoke up for the first time, her trembling voice a mere whisper, as soft and washed out as both her appearance and her paintings.

"So we won't be holding a memorial for him." There was no sarcasm in her comment.

"Inappropriate under the circumstances, don't you think?" muttered Adrian.

"But sad," Misty replied, then folded back into the safety of her shell.

Rocco looked at the walls filled with art from the interrupted show. They were already down two artists. He understood them not wanting to be associated with a murder but had hoped their loyalty would outweigh their apprehensions.

"Before we continue," he said, "is there anyone else who prefers not to stay?"

Silence.

"Good. Your support is our life blood, but our family needs to grow. Anybody know any artists who'd be interested in joining us?"

"Oh, I do," said Mary Rose, adjusting the lavender flower in her snowy hair. "My neighbor Giorgio would be a wonderful addition. He makes jewelry to sell at the swap meets. He's a silversmith and deserves better exposure. Look," she said, waving her hand in the air, "he made this ring. Very talented fellow."

Misty Waters leaned forward to look at the ring.

"He recycles broken pieces," said Mary Rose, "adds to them and creates beauty."

"A good replacement for Paloma," said Adrian. "Jewelry always sells."

"And he's a handsome devil," said Mary Rose.

That got Calypso's attention.

"Don't get optimistic," Mary Rose said to her. "He's a bit light in the loafers, if you know what I mean."

"Darn."

"And Rocco," Mary Rose continued, "he's no prima donna. He'd be a perfect fit."

"I trust your judgment."

"I'll talk to him."

"Any more ideas?"

"I can talk to a few of the art students next time I'm in Bistro Bleu. It's a hang-out for the University crowd," said Calypso. "The Bistro hangs their art. They might be students, but they're good."

"Brilliant."

"I'll get on it. They'd kiss your hairy toes to get into a real gallery." Calypso's attention drifted. She rose and started to remove her colorful collages from the wall and decorated boxes from their shelf, stacking them onto the floor. "I can't believe I didn't sell every one of them," she mumbled to no one in particular. "But I did okay, considering…"

"Misty," Rocco asked, trying to prod their resident mystery out of her silence, "do you have any ideas?"

She squirmed in her seat, uncomfortable at being the center of attention. She lowered her head and spoke. "I don't know anyone. But I'm working on some new canvases."

"Great. There's nothing else to cover, so let's get the art down and you can pick up your checks."

Misty rose and walked over to Calypso.

"Do you have a minute?"

"Sure."

"I'm looking for a home for my pet. He's a white cockatoo and his name is Baretta."

"Why would you give away such a beautiful creature?"

"He talks."

"How delightful."

"Not really. He swears like a sailor and it bothers me."

Heads turned as Calypso snorted, then muffled her laughter.

"What does he say?"

"Things I'd rather not repeat."

"I'd love to meet him."

The two women continued their conversation as Rocco started to take down Mary Rose's remaining landscapes. She was frail and the frames were heavy. There were several empty spots where her sold paintings had hung.

"You're such a gentleman," she said, approaching him. "I don't know what I'd do without you."

"And you, my darling Mary, are a true lady. Catch the door and I'll carry these to your car. It looks like you've got a healthy check coming."

"Now I can turn up the air conditioning," she said, daintily dabbing at the beads of perspiration collecting above her top lip. "That should make Sir Chesterfield happy. My fluffy feline finds the summers challenging. As do I these days."

"Tonight at The Oasis," Calypso announced with a dramatic belly dancers hip-thrust. "Come, watch me dance!" She wiggled and jiggled her multi-colored palette across the room and out the door.

One by one, the artists removed their works until the walls were freckled with nothing but empty nails and the display shelves held nothing but yesterday's dust.

* * * *

Detective Maggie Reardon tossed her cigarette butt to the pavement and ground it out with the heel of her shoe. She popped a breath mint into her mouth, then followed Jerry Montana and Aaron Iverson back into headquarters and caught up with them.

"C'mon over to my desk," she said. "I want to show you something."

"I want to go home," said Jerry.

"We rest when our work is done."

"I'm done," he said. "Call it a day."

"We've hardly begun"

"Aren't you even curious?" said Aaron. "She said it wasn't an accident. Let's see what she's got."

The two of them hovered over Maggie's chair, Jerry's arms crossed and his foot tapping impatiently as she brought up the screen on her computer. The glow from the screen mixed with the late afternoon hues that cut through the windows and across her desk.

"I've played with this over and over and no matter how I enter the calculations the results are the same."

Maggie dragged the computer's mouse from one spot to another and the two men studied the animated caricature as it performed its tricks. First it froze from different positions along the bridge railing above the javelina enclosure. Then they watched as it tumbled and did cartwheels over the railing, first from one angle and then from another.

"Gumby fall down, go boom," said Jerry. "So?"

"The point is…," she began.

"Yeah hey, I see it!" said Aaron. "No matter what you do with the guy it would have been impossible for him to go over the railing…"

"Without a helping hand."

"But there were no signs of…" said Jerry. "There wasn't a damn thing that indicated foul play and you know it. Barney Fife here is as blind as you are."

"The calculations don't lie. We've definitely got a murder on our hands. When you go back tomorrow I want you to comb every square inch of the place. The medical examiner should come up with cause of death as soon as she catches up on her backlog. That should give us a clue to the murder weapon and with luck it's out there somewhere. We need to find it."

"We?" asked Jerry sarcastically. "I don't see any dirt under your fingernails."

"I thought we had a truce," she said, rising from her chair and facing him. "Either you start treating me with respect or I'll have you written up for insubordination. You got that?"

If looks could kill, he thought, she could burn me to a crisp with those devil green eyes. "I read you, Irish," he said, knowing further comment would just fuel the flames. She was hot enough already.

"Detective Reardon to you. Why don't you practice saying that tomorrow while your sifting through all those piles of crap? It might help your perspective."

He glared at her. It was no wonder her ex boyfriend gave her a shiner and a fat lip. Instead of running the guy in, he should've given him a medal. Or paid him to finish the job he'd like to do himself. A mutually beneficial alliance if ever there was one.

"And wipe that smirk off your face."

"We're a team, aren't we?" said Aaron, trying to be diplomatic. The last thing he wanted to do as a rookie was ruffle the guy's feathers, but he was finding Jerry Montana increasingly difficult to work under.

"And it's going to take teamwork to figure this out," said Maggie.

"You betcha," said Aaron.

Maggie's phone rang and she picked it up.

"Hi Rocco," she said.

Jerry strained to hear the voice at the other end.

"Okay," she said. "I'll see you then."

She hung up the phone.

"As I was saying, we need teamwork on this."

"Right," said Jerry as he turned and walked away, squaring his shoulders so the big chip wouldn't fall off.

Aaron remained at her side as Jerry exited the front door.

"Can we talk? Confidentially?"

Maggie nodded.

"I don't like working with Jerry."

"That's no surprise."

"I know he's supposed to show me the ropes and all but he treats me like I'm some dumb-ass hayseed."

"Go on."

"Where I come from we didn't have much crime, I know that. A few break-ins, some domestic abuse calls and a book full of traffic citations. Not much of a resume. I wanted my obituary to say more than I was the cop who got the Jorgensen's cat out of the tree. Not out of ego, but because I want to make a difference. I wanted to come to a place where I could cut my teeth and prove myself, but I made a mistake."

"Don't shortchange yourself. And don't let that jerk-off discourage you."

"I'm ready to throw in the towel and go back to Minnesota. Maybe that's where I belong. I look at Jerry and think if that's what it does to somebody, if it turns me cold and hard like that...that's not how I want to be."

"No chance. Unlike Jerry, you have what it takes. You have brains and you have heart. A good cop needs both. And you're proving to be a damn good cop, even if you are a bit wet behind the ears. Give it time."

"When I saw that body this morning I damn near upchucked, like some sissy kid."

"You handled it. And better than most. Would it help to know that my first body gave me a month of nightmares?"

"Still..."

"What if I spoke with the Captain? I can't promise anything, but I'll do what I can to get you a different partner. You shouldn't have been paired with him in the first place. It's a hard enough job without having him in the mix. In the meantime I'll find some reasons to have you work closer with me."

Aaron Iverson exhaled a loud sigh of relief.

"Really? You'd do that for me?"

"Are you willing to hold out a little longer?"

"You betcha," he smiled, "and thanks!"

* * * *

The City Attorney's wife was lean and just attractive enough without being *too* pretty. Her demeanor was proper but appropriately gracious. The perfect arm candy for a man of political ambitions. The fact that she wore a simple gray sheath that accentuated her sharp hip bones, a string of baroque pearls and dress shoes didn't escape him. At an hour when most people had on their slippers and robes, she maintained the aura her husband expected of her. The perfect facade. The appropriate partner. She escorted lawyer Macy Friedman through the door and into her husband's study. The room was paneled in mahogany and law books lined the shelves next to leather bound copies of the classics. A row of classical cd's were lined up next to the expensive sound system. The soft notes of Vivaldi blended with the aroma of sweet pipe tobacco. The attorney rose from where he sat behind his large desk and held out his hand for the obligatory weak handshake. He was dressed for business. If Friedman had been carrying a baby the man would have looked around for a camera, then kissed it sweetly on the forehead. Even in the privacy of his home he remained on stage, always on the alert.

"Do sit down," he said, pointing to the leather chair that faced him from across the desk.

Friedman sat.

"Thank you," he said to his wife, indicating the door. She retreated silently, closing the door behind her.

"This is a bit unusual, don't you think?" said the attorney. "Isn't this something that could have been discussed during business hours?"

"Some things are better discussed in private."

He puffed on his pipe, then placed it in the Waterford crystal ashtray. "Go on."

"Are you familiar with Barbara Atwell?"

"I've looked through the report."

"Seventy-two hours and she has to either be charged or let go."

"I'm familiar with the law."

"Time is running out."

"Why would the La Crosse family's firm be interested? You're out of your league. Don't you usually handle their financial issues?"

"I intend to represent her. The why is beside the point."

"You're nothing but a number cruncher, Friedman." He sucked on his pipe, blowing the smoke across the desk and into Friedman's face. "She'll be formally charged in the morning."

"A wiser man would reconsider."

The attorney leaned back in his chair, reached over, and took another series of puffs from his carved Meerschaum pipe. Every item in the room was carefully placed to impress the visitor as well as himself. And he was definitely impressed with himself.

"Go on," he said.

"This is one case you'd lose and I don't think you'd be happy about it. You've got a good track record on convictions and I'm sure you'd like to keep it that way. I know your position is a mere stepping stone to grander ambitions."

He nodded.

"Your point being what exactly? The woman murdered her husband. Period."

His self-assurance was downright cocky. Friedman wanted to knock him down a peg or two.

"She's a businesswoman in the community and has been for years. She's never had as much as a parking ticket. She's clean as a Windexed window, unlike her husband who was a drug trafficker of questionable origin. Convincing a jury of self defense is a no-brainer." Then he added with a smirk, "Even for a number cruncher like me."

The attorney stared into Friedman's eyes and bristled.

"I'll take you on any day of the week," he said. "Let the games begin."

"Again, I suggest you reconsider."

There was a soft knock at the door and the wife peeked her perfectly coiffed head into the room.

"I'm sorry to interrupt," she said, ever the gracious hostess. "I was wondering if you gentlemen would like some tea or, considering the hour, perhaps a cocktail?"

"Mr. Friedman is about to leave, thanks," said the attorney, dismissing her.

"Sorry to have bothered you," she said politely and closed the door.

"There's nothing more to discuss," he said to Friedman as he rose from his chair.

"Sit back down," said Friedman. "I'm losing my patience here and you've obviously missed the point of this little visit."

"I'll sit when I feel like it."

"Suit yourself," he smiled. "I'll spell it out for you. You wouldn't have the position you have without La Crosse support. And the only reason you have their support is because they're friends with your wife."

"Your point being?"

"You'll never reach your goals without La Crosse money and it's the only reason you've gotten as far as you have. I'm the messenger and the message is this: I guarantee that if you don't cooperate and drop this case your well will run dry and you can kiss your dream of living in the governor's mansion goodbye."

"Is that a threat?"

"The La Crosse family doesn't need threats. They state facts."

"I'll take your suggestion under consideration," he said. "We're finished here."

"Wise decision." Friedman was ignored as he held out his hand. "And don't think for a minute that I don't know your dirty little secrets. How long do you think she'd stand quietly at your side if she knew what you were up to?"

"You can show yourself out," said the attorney.

CHAPTER SEVEN

Cold Margaritas and Hot Kisses

The young woman pulled back the curtain in the darkened room, slid open the window and looked up. The sky looked like an old torn mattress, it's stuffing scattered across the ceiling. Twilight flirted with darkness and the air was thick with the aroma of approaching rain. The motel parking lot was nearly full. She read the out of state plates on the cars and held up her fingers, counting how many of those places they'd been through. Their travels were her geography lessons but there had been so many places that it was nothing but a blur of ever changing landscapes and generic motel rooms for as far back as she could remember. As hard as she tried, she was unable to take her memory back beyond the days they began traveling the roads and routes that led to no particular destination. Her eyes scanned the lot in search of his old green Chevy. He should have been back by now. Maybe he found a good job today that was running late. That would mean more money in their pocket but she missed him and needed him to fill the emptiness of the room.

Tracks of rain slid down the dusty window pane.

She closed the window and locked it.

She flicked on the light, turned back into the room, and ran her hand across the top of the television. It was no longer warm so he'd never know she'd been watching, not for sure. She still wore her tattered nightgown from the night before. What was the point of getting dressed when you had nowhere to go? Her stomach growled, interrupting her thoughts. She was hungry. She was tired of nibbling on dry cereal and even drier jerky. If he'd had a good day maybe he'd take her out to celebrate. Or bring home something special for them to eat in the room. She pulled the nightgown over her head and flung it across the room, exposing her thin, girlish figure. Looking at her reflection in the mirror, for a fleeting moment, she wondered who she was. At times she felt like a caged hamster, forgotten and alone.

But he'd come through the door and everything would be right again.

She walked to the pole that hung between the room and the bath that served as a makeshift closet and pulled her ragged prairie skirt from its hanger. She stepped into it and slipped it over her hips then reached up to the shelf and grabbed a mismatched top. If he was going to take her out she'd be ready. When she finished dressing she sat down in the middle of the bed, wrapping herself in the silence.

And waited.

Outside, hidden by the encroaching shadows of night, the tall young man also waited. He pulled a cell phone from his pocket and punched in eleven numbers, listened to the static as it reached across the country to his other world.

Someone picked up at the other end.

His voice quivered as he spoke.

"She's been found."

* * * *

The magic fingers of Dave Brubeck tickled the piano keys, the mellow tones flowing from the speakers and filling the house. Maggie Reardon placed the bowl of Prowler's cat food onto the floor. He rubbed his thanks against her leg, then dug into it as if he hadn't eaten for a week. She turned and headed for the bedroom.

"You're on your own tonight," she yelled back to him. "Mama's got a date."

She tightened the sash on her bathrobe, still damp from her shower, and stared into the closet. One long row of clothes looked back at her. She hadn't a clue what to wear. All Rocco La Cross had told her was to come hungry. Were they going to a restaurant? Staying in? Did it even matter? Just keep it simple, she thought, pulling a pair of charcoal slacks from their hanger. Don't look too anxious. And don't look like you're trying too hard. She took a plain beige blouse and tossed it onto the bed. Maggie opened a bureau drawer filled with undergarments and shook her head. A small stack of frayed but practical cotton briefs, the kind her mother had said not to be caught in should she get in an accident. Mothers said things like that. Well, she certainly didn't want to get caught in them should things progress tonight with Rocco. If they did, she was ready. She fished around in the drawer and pulled lace trimmed black bikini panties from where they hid in the back with a matching girly bra, the sales tags still attached. She wondered why she'd ever bought them. It would take more than a bit of skimpy Victoria's Secret to make herself irresistible. And even with the best effort, she'd never measure up to those beyond perfect models they used in their ads, with their long giraffe legs and perfect midriffs. Where the hell did they find them? In some junior high school? Nobody over eighteen could look that perfect. Skimpy undies weren't her usual preference, cotton was definitely more comfortable, but tonight she wanted the right ammunition, loaded and ready.

Just in case.

She reached into the top drawer, took out a pair of cuticle scissors and snipped off the tags.

The thought of Rocco seeing her in those made her feel silly.

And apprehensive.

She put them on, looked in the mirror and shrugged. A boyish figure masked in lace was still a boyish figure. It was just wrapped prettier, like a gift from a discount store topped with a pretty bow that promised something special but failed to deliver. Hell, it is what it is and you work with the tools you've been given.

"Besides," she said aloud, "it's not like Rocco La Crosse has the physique of Charles Atlas."

Prowler entered the room with his usual growl and looked up at her, beads of gravy dripping from his furry chin.

"No cop badge tonight," she said.

She blew the dust from off the small jewelry box that sat on top of the bureau and lifted the lid. It held a few pieces that had belonged to her mother. Maggie chose a vintage piece and pinned it to her blouse. It was a large carved cameo, with smaller cameos at each side surrounded by fresh water pearls and brass scroll work.

"Thanks mom," she said. "I remember how you glowed when you wore that."

When she was five she'd asked her mother if she could have it when she died. Of course a child thinks their parents will live forever and never, ever die. The death of a dime store goldfish was enough for a child to handle. She had asked her mother why she wore it every day. She said Maggie's father had bought it for her on their Italian honeymoon, in the small town of Caserta near Naples. And she wore it to remind herself how much they loved each other and to keep that love as fresh and wonderful as it was the day he'd bought it for her. Her mother had told her she was conceived on their honeymoon, but as bad as she was at math Maggie suspected she'd been in the oven before their wedding vows were ever spoken.

She missed them, but the aura of their love still filled the house and gave her comfort. She ran her fingers through her short hair and pulled up the spikes. The foundation almost hid the fading bruises under her eyes. She added a subtle touch of eye shadow. Her mouth was barely swollen now and it no longer hurt as she applied pale lipstick. A dab of perfume in the hollow of her neck finished the job.

"That'll do," she said. "With a bit of luck I'll be home late." Prowler released his muffled growl in response, then jumped onto the bed and settled onto her pillow. Half way out the door she stopped and turned back, returning to the living room. She grabbed a brown paper bag, picked up her pack of smokes and headed for her car.

* * * *

The young man held the cell phone to his ear, listening to the voice at the other end.

"It's been a long time coming," he said. "I'll call back in a day or two and arrange for your flight."

He disconnected, wiped the rain drops from the phone and shoved it into his pocket. The motel room curtain was lit from behind by a faint lamplight. He wondered what she was doing and how long it would take her to venture out by herself. He resisted the urge to knock on the door and finally face her.

What would he say? He'd practiced that moment over and over, but the right words still failed to come.

The timing had to be right, no matter how long he had to wait. If nothing else, the long search had taught him patience. How could his first face to face with her appear accidental? A light bulb went off in his head and he walked into the motel office and leaned his elbows onto the counter.

"I'd like a room," he said to the clerk, a middle aged woman who looked like she drank too much and had an aversion to bath water. He leaned back from the faint aroma of stale perspiration and alcohol fumes and waited.

The clerk pulled up a screen on her computer and studied it.

"You're in luck," she finally said. "There's one room left."

He filled out the registration card and took the room key as she slid it across the counter. The run-down place was no Ritz-Carlton, but with luck the room would be cleaner than the desk clerk. He took the key and walked the long block to where his car was parked. He drove it into the motel parking lot, pulled a few belongings from the trunk and headed to the room. It was only two doors down from where the girl was staying. Luck was on his side. It would be easy to cross her path now, unsuspected.

* * * *

Maggie Reardon dodged the raindrops as she walked up the path that led to Rocco La Crosse's front door. She smiled at the metal statues along the way, his creations made of scrap metal and old plumbing fixtures and had to laugh at one with an upside-down water spigot welded between its legs like it was *really* glad to see her. It stood next to a female figure, breasts created from dented and corroded metal funnels. They weren't offensive in any way, despite their saucy trimmings. They were whimsical and meant to evoke a smile. They succeeded.

She stood at the mammoth door of his pseudo-Spanish Colonial estate, juggling the items that filled her hands. Before she could free a hand to knock or ring the bell, the door opened. The aroma of garlic and cumin and cayenne greeted her, along with the faintest hint of Old Spice and a smiling Rocco. He had trimmed a bit of scruff from his beard and had his long hair pulled into a pony tail at the back of his neck. Instead of his usual t-shirt he was wearing a bright red and white striped rugby shirt with long sleeves that covered his tattoo-etched arms. The shirt looked like it was fresh from the store and his un-faded jeans still held their original folds.

He had gone out of his way to look good for her.

Maggie looked behind her, taking in the million dollar view of the Santa Catalina mountains and the panoramic view of Tucson, it's lights glistening through the rain and spreading like lake water beneath the carpet of murky sky.

"Let me help you with those," he said, taking the heavy paper sack from her. "Don't just stand there, come on in."

She took a deep breath and stepped across the threshold.

"I hope you don't mind us eating in," he said as she sat her purse next to the hallway table where he had placed the paper sack. The table was heavily carved in the same style as the house's architecture and appeared to be a true antique rather than a reproduction.

"I like to cook," he said. "I like the creative process. And the challenge."

"Just one more surprise from the enigmatic Mr. La Crosse."

"If you like to read you'll find I'm really an open book," he said.

"But a very complex one filled with sub-plots and twists."

"And a few surprises," he finished. "One of my specialties is in the oven."

Maggie faced him, standing a little too close.

"I'm ready for chapter one," she flirted, then took an awkward step backwards and changed the subject. "It smells wonderful. I'd guess something south of the border by the mix of spices."

"You have a good nose."

"I'm a detective. It's my job."

"Tonight I'd like you to just be Maggie." He looked at the bag he'd set on the hallway table.

"That was pretty heavy. Did you bring an arsenal just in case I get out of hand?"

"I almost forgot," she said, reaching over and handing it to him. "A gift for the host."

Rocco opened it and smiled. It was filled with old hose nozzles, washers and bolts, pieces of broken wire.

"Thank you, Maggie. I can make something special from these. Thoughtful and perfect."

He looked down at the tile floor, unsure of what to say next. He scratched his beard, betraying his nervousness.

"We're both feeling a bit awkward," she said. "Let's kick that big elephant out of the room so we can relax."

Maggie reached out and held her hands along the sides of his face, leaned in and gave him a kiss on the lips. The kiss was soft and sweet and gentle and tasted like wintergreen promises.

"There," she said. "The elephant is gone."

"Wow."

"I've seen the room with the leather furniture and the bookshelves, back when I was questioning you about Barbara and Armando. Why not give me the tour?"

He led her through the den with it's ceiling high bookshelves and through the glass doors that led to the back patio.

"The rain's coming down harder," he said. "Maybe we should…"

"A little rain isn't going to stop me."

They stepped out onto the covered patio and stood side by side like old friends. The patio was nearly as large as Maggie's entire house, complete with outdoor kitchen and sturdy furniture and a fireplace. Just beyond it was a large swimming pool framed by the Tucson mountains that loomed beyond the wall of giant boulders and cacti that edged the property line. She'd never been to one, but her only comparison was some fancy resort that catered to the ultra-rich.

"I'm impressed," she said. "It's breathtaking."

"That wasn't my goal," he said. "It looked like this when I bought the place." He shrugged and smiled. "Okay, maybe I wanted to impress you just a little."

"Do you remember the first time we met each other? At The Mosaic Gallery? When you pulled up in that beat up van?"

"How could I forget? You looked like a hard-nosed cop if ever I saw one."

His paunch had led the way as he walked toward her. With the tattoos, pony tail and piercings he'd looked like an outlaw biker who'd downed one too many six-packs.

"You were disheveled with worry plastered across your face. And you comforted Barbara and Adrian like a protective father. That's what impressed me. That and your eyes." There was no doubt that electricity had passed between them when they first looked at each other.

"I like a woman who can see past the window dressing."

Maggie was willing to bet he'd had his share of gold diggers, but she also bet that he could smell them out and toss them aside with equal aplomb. Being monied definitely had its down-side, for a man or a woman. One was never sure if some suitor's aim was genuine or if money was the main attraction.

"Any news on Barbara?" he asked, thinking of his friend sitting in a jail cell.

"I was going to ask you the same thing. Have you heard anything from your lawyer friend?"

"Not yet. But he knows his business and he knows where the bodies are buried, if you get my drift."

"He's got the right ammunition for the right war."

"Exactly."

The night air was muggy but held the hint of a chill.

They went back inside.

"It smells done," he said, leading her through the dining room and into the kitchen. It didn't escape her attention that he had set a beautiful table with wrought iron candlesticks, not fancy but elegant in their simplicity. The kitchen was huge but warm and homey. A large island in the middle was topped with a thick slab of smoothed mesquite wood and the counter tops and back splash were adorned with ornate, hand-painted Mexican tiles.

Rocco opened the oven door, then slammed it shut. "Not quite yet. I'd say about ten more minutes." He walked over to the blender and pulled out a bottle, then opened the fridge and scooped out some ice. "I think a frozen Margarita is in order, don't you?" He whirled it up like a well trained bartender, poured the frothy mixture and handed her a glass trimmed in salt. "Let's retreat to the den."

She followed him and they sat in comfy leather chairs, staring into the glowing fire that was sandwiched between the tall shelves filled with books on every imaginable subject.

"This is my favorite room," he said. "Except for my outdoor studio where I work. Both places relax me, no end."

Rocco hit the play button on the stereo and an old Julio Iglesias tape started working its magic, the romantic lyrics blending perfectly with the aromas from the kitchen.

Maggie was feeling more at ease and relaxed than she had in a long time. Marty the ex was behind bars where he belonged, her old case looked like it could wrap up with a happy ending and she had a new case to focus on. But that could wait until morning. Tonight she wanted to concentrate on Rocco. The detective in her was more than curious as to where things might lead.

She was ready to let her guard down and allow optimism in.

And she was prepared to gamble, let the chips fall where they may.

In unison, the two potential lovers sipped their Margaritas and leaned back in their chairs.

"I could sit like this forever," Maggie said. "This room is like, I don't know how to explain it. It's like a prayer to the gods of serenity."

* * * *

The warmth of Rocco's special enchiladas filled their stomachs as he and Maggie pushed their chairs back from the table and rose.

"You're one hell of a cook, Mr. La Crosse."

"I'll refill our Margaritas," he said as he headed to the kitchen. "I think we should let the meal settle before we tackle dessert."

"You made dessert?"

"Just something light. Flan. Whipped cream."

She followed, handing him her empty glass.

The mixer's whirr danced a salsa through the room then stopped abruptly. He re-rimmed their glasses with salt, poured the heavenly broth and handed her a glass. They clinked them together, then let the liquid chill slide down their throats.

An awkward silence filled the space between them, pheromones mixing with the aroma of Old Spice and enchilada sauce and animal attraction.

"It's time for the rest of the house tour," he said.

Maggie was torn. The logical side of her brain begged for caution. She was still recovering from her last mistake and needed a break before venturing forward. Some breathing time. She felt like there was an angel on one shoulder and a devil on the other, each one arguing their point and whispering in her ears. She mentally listed her past mistakes, weighing the pros and cons. Then she told herself that when you get bucked off that horse, the best thing to do is get right back on. She'd been waiting for what seemed like forever to test the waters with Rocco. He was puzzling and complex, he was simple and straight-forward. He oozed something she found irresistible. The tequila buzz relaxed her just enough to let her impulsive nature win out.

"Let's start with the bedroom," she said.

Rocco leaned in and kissed her gently on the lips.

CHAPTER EIGHT

Snags

Maggie Reardon's last intention was to spend the night with Rocco La Crosse, at least not in the literal sense. Their lovemaking had been sweet but so intense that she had settled into his arms, exhausted. Despite the hairs that tickled her nose, his chest was a welcome pillow against her face. Before she knew it she'd fallen asleep, their bodies forming pieces of a jigsaw puzzle that fit perfectly together. One more surprise from Mr. La Crosse. And a very pleasant one. His skills as a lover were matched only by his culinary talents and his artistic creativity.

Her sleep had been deep and dreamless for the first time in a long time.

She awakened with a jolt, passed on Rocco's offer of coffee and ran out the door. She drove home with a smile on her face and optimism in her heart. Her hasty retreat left Rocco wearing a quick kiss on the forehead and a look of confusion on his face, but she had no time to go into explanations. It was a work day and she couldn't afford to be late. She didn't have an artist's luxury of sleeping til noon if the mood struck or inspiration didn't, let alone the freedom of relaxing over a cup of coffee. Her job called the shots and the time clock was her canvas.

Maggie flew through her front door, fed Prowler and gave her teeth a quick brushing. She stepped into fresh clothes and strapped on her gun belt, concealing it under a light-weight cotton jacket. There was just enough time for her morning stop to see Carlos before she went to headquarters. She was looking forward to filling him in. Talking to him was better than sharing with a girlfriend over a bottle of Zinfandel any day. Female friendships remained a mystery to her and she found their chatter frivolous. She didn't care about fashions or celebrity gossip. They yawned at her tales of bad guys and gun battles. They gossiped about strangers, and even worse they gossiped about each other. If she hadn't bowed out they would have excluded her anyway.

She didn't fit their mold nor did she want to.

Men weren't great conversationalists, but when they did say something it tended to be honest and direct. Unless they were bent on seduction, of course, but that's just the way they were assembled. She found them easier, despite her occasional lapses in judgment. Cupid confused her and she found him as much of a trickster as the Norse god Loki.

But this time she was ready to fight him head on.

This time it might be worth it.

She rushed out the door and into her car, daydreaming as the car followed its usual route.

Maggie pulled into a parking space and exited her car. A lone rain cloud clung stubbornly to a distant mountain top and the morning air was filled with pollen and humidity.

She inhaled, sneezed and entered the mini-mart.

She stopped cold.

Carlos wasn't at the register.

He was always there, but today she was face to face with a young man who looked like a gang banger. Her cop antenna rose and she instinctively reached down and rested her hand on the butt of her gun. Was he robbing the place? He wore a black t-shirt and low-slung khakis but appeared unshaken by her presence. It wasn't until she looked into his eyes that she relaxed.

He had Carlos's eyes, soft and gentle.

But where was Carlos? She imagined the worst.

"How may I help you, señora?" the young man asked politely.

She searched for words. She couldn't lose Carlos. He was her anchor. She was still trying to come to terms with the loss of her parents. It was a long time ago, but made no more sense now than it had when she was a teenager. To be blinded by a haboob? A violent desert dust storm? Perhaps for some unfortunate Arab in the middle of the Sahara, but for her parents? Cancer would have made more sense. People got blind-sided by that devil all the time. Even little children. The grim reaper had a way of wrapping himself in irony and popping up with the most unexpected of demises. She saw it every day but his nasty bag of tricks never failed to surprise her.

"Carlos," she said. "Where is Carlos?"

She was afraid of the answer. Was he sick? Was he in an accident? She was on the verge of panic.

"He had something to attend do," he replied calmly. "I am his nephew Ramon."

"Maggie."

"You are Maggie Reardon! He speaks of you so often that I feel I already know you and that you are one of our family."

Ramon reached across the counter and gave her hand a hearty shake.

"Is he alright? Is something wrong?" She asked.

"No, no Miss Reardon, he is fine. There was just something he needed to do today. Pardon me if I'm a bit slow at my job. I've never done this before but my Uncle Carlos says I am the only one he can truly trust."

Ramon's English was measured and correct, which indicated he was probably born this side of the border despite the definite Spanish speech pattern. He was polite and he was charming but he was also determined to keep Carlos's whereabouts a mystery. But why?

"When will he be back?"

"*Mañana*. He will be back tomorrow. I see worry in your eyes. There is no need for worry."

His smile was so like that of his uncle, but held stubborn determination. If he'd been sitting across from her in the interrogation room she'd still have gotten zilch from him, whether she was playing good cop or bad cop.

Maggie walked down the aisle and poured an extra large black coffee.

She returned to the counter and watched as Ramon fumbled with the cash register.

"Forgive my slowness," he said. "This is new for me."

The grime imbedded beneath his fingernails told Maggie he was more comfortable under the chassis of a car than dealing with the public.

"You're doing fine," she said.

"*Gracias.*"

"It was nice to have met you, Ramon." He handed her a receipt and her change and another smile.

"Are you sure he'll be back tomorrow? Are you sure there's nothing wrong?"

"I will tell him you asked after him. That will bring him joy. And I am glad to have finally met his special Detective Maggie Reardon."

* * * *

The Captain stood before the seated officers, winding up his morning pep talk. Jerry Montana looked at her with his usual smirk as Maggie and Aaron Iverson nodded at each other. Montana looked like the cat that ate the canary and she swore he did it just to irritate her. Animosity covered him head to toe like oozing muck, dripping from his eyes and obliterating what might otherwise have been a good-looking man. The ugliness that festered inside of him escaped through his every pore. He reminded her of some crazy that opened fire in a crowded room, a walking time-bomb ready to go off. She wondered if everyone sensed it or if it was just her imaginings because he found pleasure in aiming his venom in her direction.

Maggie dismissed him from her thoughts and returned her attention to the Captain.

"We've got to make some headway on the body from the Desert Museum," he said. "And we need to find him a name other than John Doe. Somebody's got to know who this guy was."

"Welcome to the Hotel Javelina," Jerry mumbled the words to the melody of Hotel California by the Eagles.

No one heard him except Maggie and Aaron, who both shot him a dirty look.

"Any questions?" asked the Captain.

Silence.

"That's it then."

The noise of shuffling papers and the squeaking of leather holsters followed everyone as they rose and headed out to confront another day.

"Hold up, Detective Reardon," the Captain called.

Maggie turned and faced him.

"Yes sir?"

"We need to talk."

Jerry Montana looked back over his shoulder and gave her a wink before heading out the door.

She walked across the room and stood before the Captain, expecting to be chewed out regarding the lack of progress on the Desert Museum case.

"We're doing the best we can, sir. And they're backed up, so I'm still waiting on the autopsy report."

"It takes as long as it takes," he said with a dismissive wave. "Just keep on top of it."

"Yes, sir," she said, turning to leave.

"I'm not finished."

"Sorry."

"Something has come to my attention that we need to discuss. I'll get to the point. You've been more than lax on proper procedure regarding the murder at the Mosaic Gallery."

"I don't understand."

"I hear you've been fraternizing with witnesses. You know better than that Detective. It's something that could influence testimony when Barbara Atwell comes to trial. If the judge knew you were maintaining an intimate relationship with a witness anything you'd say regarding the case would be jeopardized. And your testimony would be thrown out right along with you. We have a reputation and I expect you to maintain it." He paused. "You disappoint me. I thought you were more professional than that."

How could he have known about last night? Unless...

"What, was that creep Montana following me? He was, wasn't he?"

"The source is irrelevant."

"The source is everything."

"My instinct is to put you on temporary leave, but you'd probably spend it with that den of bohemians. We both know you have a problem following orders."

"Only when they don't make sense, sir."

"Consider yourself warned. Distance yourself until this is wrapped up in a neat little bow. After that I could care less about your private life."

"Understood."

"Good."

"Sir?"

"Yes?"

"I don't understand why he wasn't fired a long time ago. He's a loose cannon. He's certainly not professional. He's rude and his work is sloppy. He's hateful and he's just not right. He's a Mexican who hates Mexicans and makes no secret of it. If that isn't a red flag to his instability I don't know what is. His judgment is clouded and he's trouble waiting to happen."

"Sit down. There's things about Jerry you'll never understand, but this might help. You haven't been here long enough to know the skinny on him and I think it's time you knew."

The two sat down in the empty room and faced each other.

"Jerry Montana used to be one of the best cops we had."

"Not any more. Not by a long shot."

"Agreed."

"Then why haven't you weeded him out?"

"Long before you were hired on, Jerry was a good cop, married to a good wife, the whole bag. Esperanza was his love. One day Esperanza drove down to visit with her sister who owned a rancho with her husband just this side of the Nogales border. They were a close-knit family and visited back and forth all the time. She and her sister took the horses out to ride around the property that day."

Maggie squirmed in her seat. The last thing she was interested in was the history of Jerry Montana.

"I'll keep it short. They were waylaid by crossers. Not the poor souls searching for a better life. The women probably crossed paths with some drug mules. Anyway, Esperanza and her sister were pulled from their horses. They were beaten and their horses stolen. Esperanza was raped and her throat was cut ear to ear. Somehow her sister survived but she was never the same after that."

"That's horrible."

"The killers were never caught."

"No surprise there. They worm through the underbrush like rattlesnakes."

"And they're just as slippery. Anyway, that's why he is the way he is."

"But he remarried. Wouldn't that mean he moved on?"

"The wife tries. I give her credit for that much, but it's hard to measure up to a memory."

"Why does she put up with him? Word is he doesn't treat her right."

"She's young and white and not too bright. But her heart's in the right place. She thought she could fix him, but nothing can wring out that anger and pain. Not even her."

"You can fix a broken leg, but you can't fix broken people. If they're broken they're broken. All the more reason to get rid of him."

"It comes down to loyalty. He was good once and this job is all he has. I don't think he could handle losing it."

"I sympathize, honestly I do. I've experienced loss myself, but you don't see me taking it out on the world."

"You don't have to like him, just-I don't know. Just try to understand a little."

"He's annoying and he's unstable."

I've known Jerry a long time and I've never seen him hurt anybody but himself."

"You want me to be a cop or a damn social worker?"

"Sometimes we have to be a little of each."

"I'm not heartless sir, but I am practical."

"Just cut him some slack."

"I respect you, more than you know. If it weren't for your confidence in me I'd never had made detective. I'm thankful for that, believe me. But giving him a free pass could come back to bite you in the behind. Sir."

"I doubt that. Now, back to the other issue."

"Honestly? Some of those gallery people have become friends. I like them and they're good people. Personally, I don't think Barbara Atwell belongs behind bars, but I did the job I was expected to do. And I don't sneak around tailing fellow officers."

"Give it a rest. Distance yourself from them. All of them. At least for now."

Maggie nodded, rose and headed for the door.

"That's an order."

She nodded.

"And Detective Reardon?"

"Yes sir?"

"You're the best damn detective I've got. Don't be going all touchy-feely on me."

He should talk, she thought to herself as she pushed through the door, slamming head on into the city attorney. He carried a scowl on his face and a briefcase in his hand and shoved past her without as much as an acknowledgment or an excuse me and went inside. Today he would officially charge Barbara Atwell with the murder of her husband Armando. Maggie had done her job and he was doing his, but that fact didn't help much.

Maggie and authority had always butted heads, yet the profession she'd chosen put her in a position of authority. It was a game of tug o' war. No matter which side won the other lost, leaving her dangling somewhere in the middle.

And now she had to back off from Rocco and play nice with Montana.

The game was getting tougher and the rope was starting to feel like a noose.

CHAPTER NINE

Camouflage

The sound of her own stomach growling woke up the young woman in the motel room. Light filtered through the gap in the closed curtains and spread across the empty side of the bed. She sat upright, pushed the hair from her face and rubbed her eyes, trying to get her bearings.

He hadn't returned.

She was alone and she didn't know what to do.

Her heart pounded. She was scared.

Had something horrible happened to him?

He'd told her how dangerous the world was.

Or had he just abandoned her?

No, he'd never, ever do that.

For as far back as she could remember, he loved her.

She didn't know which felt worse, her fear of abandonment or the gnawing hunger in her empty stomach.

The phone on the side table beckoned her, trying to coax her toward it. Just pick me up, it said. Call for help.

She wanted to call the police, to tell them he had disappeared, but he had told her that the police were no better than the gestapo in Nazi Germany. She had no idea what the gestapo was, let alone Nazi Germany, but she understood the tone in his voice when he'd told her that. They were danger and they were to be avoided. That was all she needed to know.

She rose from the bed and walked over to her box of breakfast cereal, turning it upside-down and giving it a shake. Eight colorful puffs fell to the floor, speckling the dingy carpet like tiny flowers. She shook the box again. It was empty. She hurled it across the room and threw herself onto the bed.

There was no one to hear her sobs or to dry her tears.

* * * *

Detective Maggie Reardon reached across her desk and picked up the ringing phone.

"Yes, put it through."

She listened, inserting the occasional *uh huh* between pauses.

"Just leave it where it is," she said. "Yes, it might well be. I'll send someone out there to pick it up. And thanks for being so observant. We want to wind this up as much as you do."

She hung up the phone, then punched in Montana's cell number. He and Aaron were likely already on the Museum grounds.

"Jerry, Maggie Reardon here. No, I'm not calling about that, you creep. This is business. Are you two out there yet?"

"We're just pulling in."

"There's a green Chevy parked in the lot."

Jerry made a snide remark.

"We can talk about that later," she said. "Do you see the car?"

The phone went silent as she waited.

"An old puke green junker? Yeah, I can see it from here."

"It might be the clue we're looking for. I need you to take photos before the tow truck gets there. Wait there until they do. And don't touch anything."

She hung up before he could respond and punched in an extension.

"I just got a call from the Desert Museum. Seems there's a car that's been parked there awhile. It was there last night and it was still there this morning. I think there's a good chance it belongs to our John Doe. I need a tow to bring it in so forensics can go over it inch by inch. And give me a heads up when it gets here."

She listened to the voice at the other end.

"Look for an old green Chevy. Montana and Iverson are already on scene and waiting."

Maggie returned to shuffling through papers and digesting her earlier conversation with the Captain. Even Rocco must have his limits. Backing off meant goodbye. Nobody wants to be stuck in second place. And the men in her life had always come in second. She worried about Carlos. And then there was Jerry Montana. His trouble-making just added fuel to the fire that was building inside her. He'd followed her. It was creepy, like having a stalker. What kind of detective was she that she hadn't spotted him? He'd always resented her and made her uncomfortable, but she'd underestimated just how low he could go. Her anger was building. She picked up a sharpened pencil and hurled it upward toward the acoustic ceiling. It stuck like a well-aimed javelin to the tile above her head, adding one more spear to the small forest of stubs. It was a safe way to let off steam, although she'd rather have aimed it straight at Montana's heart.

If anyone had noticed the overhead collection of pencil stubs they'd said nothing. It reminded her of the high school librarian who'd watched the collection of spit balls build like snowflakes against the window pane. Maggie would get the occasional scowl, but she'd never been caught. She'd learned early on that you don't act on hunches and suspicions, you act on evidence. The librarian might have suspected, but Maggie was too fast for her. In the teenagers eyes, there was no harm done. It wasn't like it was graffiti. She'd never have actually defaced anything. Spit balls, unlike bullets in a riddled body, washed off like nothing had ever been there.

It would be awhile before the car was towed in. It would be even longer before forensics could go through it, dust it for prints and check out anything else they might find. It was unlikely they'd find any blood. John Doe was definitely killed on the bridge over the javelina enclosure. No way somebody could have carted that dead weight through a public place unnoticed. It was equally surprising he could be killed on the spot without somebody witnessing it, but that's how it was adding up. It took a lot of chutzpah, or a lot of anger, to take a chance like that. She'd stay put until she got the call regarding the car and hoped it would prove to have belonged to the corpse they'd found in the cactus.

She wanted to give him a name.

It would be a starting point.

In the meantime, there was plenty of catch up paperwork. She shuffled through the forms, but her mind was on Rocco La Crosse. Sooner or later she'd have to tell him it was over. She picked up the phone and dialed his number. Might as well get it over with and move on.

"Rocco here."

"Hi, it's Maggie."

"You sound down, but it's good to hear your voice. I wondered if I'd ever hear from you again. You ran out of here this morning like you were on fire. Was last night that bad?"

"Bad? It was perfect. In every way."

"Glad to hear I haven't lost my touch."

His voice was soft and sexy, like the actor John Gavin in the old movies.

The thought of Rocco touching her sent goose bumps up her arm.

"I apologize for racing out like I did, but I was late."

"Business first, right?"

"You've got me pegged."

"I was wondering if—"

"We've got to talk."

Rocco groaned. "You know that's the one sentence no one ever wants to hear. It's never good."

"No, it's not good. I got chewed out by the Captain this morning. I've got direct orders to stay away from you and to distance myself from anyone connected to the gallery or Barbara's case."

"Why should your personal life matter to him?"

"It's complicated. Everything is. But the bottom line is that it could interfere with the testimony when it goes to trial. It could sully my credibility. I get it, I just don't like it."

"Either do I."

"I care about you. I was ready to take a chance, Rocco. I'm so sorry it has to end like this."

"End? Why should it end?"

"I told you why."

Maggie wanted to cry, but she didn't.

"Maggie, Maggie, Maggie. It's not the end, not if you don't want it to be. This situation isn't going to last forever, even if it does end up going to trial, which I seriously doubt."

"You're an optimist. But it could be a long time and it's not fair to you."

"I waited a long time for last night and it was worth it. I love your company. It's nice finding out who you are when you're not hiding behind your badge. Just think of it as a bump in the road. I think I'm capable of waiting longer if that's the way it has to be."

"Are you sure? I don't think having to deal with me is ever going to be easy."

"You're worth some waiting. Last night proved that. Hey, I'm more than willing to take a break between chapter one and chapter two. I've barely cracked the book but I have to see it through and I'm curious to see how it ends." Pause. "If it ends."

This wasn't the response she expected.

"I always thought that if something was right it would be easy."

"Nothing about you is easy. It won't be fun, but I'll back off and wait to hear from you. Who knows? Maybe next time I'll cook Italian and we can down a jug of cheap Chianti so we can tolerate each others garlic breath."

"I'm sure going to miss you."

* * * *

The Captain and the City Attorney faced each other like two pit bulls ready to do battle. The Captain's blood pressure was rising and his face was turning red. The little blue veins popping out on his forehead didn't escape the attorney's attention. It was proof he held the upper hand. The attorney stubbornly stood his ground, waving the papers in his hand, cool and composed and sure of himself.

"You've got to be shitting me," said the Captain.

"This is my call."

"She murdered her husband, we've collected the evidence, what else do you need?"

"Not enough to convict."

"Shouldn't that be up to a jury?"

"And how will it look when she's exonerated? There's enough question marks on this one that getting a conviction will be damn near impossible. Add to that the community outrage and the negative press. You've got a lifelong Tucsonan who defended herself against a drug dealer. It doesn't matter if it was her own husband or a total stranger. Are you getting the picture?"

The captain had to give the city attorney credit, though he sure as hell wasn't going to give him the satisfaction of saying it aloud. After the cops did their job the guy usually wrapped it all up in a pretty bow and the perp went to prison where he belonged.

"The picture I'm seeing," he said, "is a man determined to maintain his conviction record. And I question your motivation."

"See it any way you want. There will be no charges filed against Barbara Atwell. Just an unfortunate situation that got out of control. It was self-defense. Period."

"We've put a lot of time and manpower into this. Come on, he wasn't even facing her when she hit him with that death blow."

"It's too weak and it won't fly. Get her walking papers in order and send her home."

The Captain looked at him with his meanest bad cop look. There was no intimidating him. The guy wouldn't flinch. It was like trying to stare down some animal who refused to blink.

"There's more to this, isn't there?"

"I don't like insinuations. I know my job. And you know all you need to know," he answered. "Just cut her loose."

He headed for the door, then turned and faced the Captain.

"It's my call," he repeated, slowly as if speaking to a dense child. He straightened his silk tie and was gone before the Captain could respond. Just as well.

"Arrogant s.o.b.," he muttered under his breath, then reached for the phone. The guy was good at his job but he was no Perry Mason. Not by a long shot.

"Reardon, get your butt in here. Now."

* * * *

She could tell by the look in his eyes that he was not a happy camper. Detective Maggie Reardon stood before the Captain waiting to get chewed out again. She'd thought their earlier conversation was over but he was definitely poised for round two.

"You had something to do with this, didn't you?" It was more of an accusation than a question. He looked like he'd just been through world war three, perspiration gathering on his flushed face as he spoke.

She just looked at him, puzzled.

"Barbara Atwell," he said.

"What about her?"

"Don't tell me you don't know what's going on or that you didn't have a hand in it. I didn't get to be Captain by not having good instincts and I'm smelling a foul odor."

"I'm sorry sir, but I don't have a clue what you're talking about."

"I just had an unwelcome visitor and he wasn't the bearer of good news."

"I saw him leave. Smug and rude as ever."

"At least we agree on something."

"What's going on?"

"There will be no charges filed against Barbara Atwell. We're cutting her loose."

Maggie did her best not to smile or exhale a sigh of relief. Rocco's magic had worked once again. It made her wonder exactly what kind of dirt his connections had on the City Attorney. It must be some heavy stuff to get results this fast.

"I'm...surprised," she said. "We put a lot of work into this."

"Don't shit me, Reardon. I can see it in those bright green eyes. You are not disappointed."

"Why would you think I was involved in any way?"

"Hmmm, let me see," he said. "The detective working the case gets all chummy with every heathen connected to the gallery and the crime. Then she gets...let's say *extra chummy* with a character named Rocco La Crosse. La Crosse, mind you. You put the family name La Crosse into the mix and you've got Tucson money and Tucson power and

Tucson clout. And a La Crosse who is very close to the murder suspect. Can you see how things are starting to add up here?"

"You have a point, but you know me well enough to know I'd never intentionally do anything to jeopardize a case or an investigation in any way. I'm professional and I take my job seriously."

"I think you stumbled over your heart on this one."

"Honestly sir, I knew Rocco was contacting his lawyer, but I had no hand in any of it, regardless of how I felt on a personal level."

"I'll take your word on it, only because you've never failed me in the past. But I really think your emotions have gotten in the way and clouded your vision. Don't let it happen again."

Maggie thought a long time before she spoke.

"Thanks," she began. "You're the last person I want to disappoint. Or cross. You've known me since day one. As a young rookie I saw the world in black and white. There were the bad guys and there were the good guys. I wanted to nail the bad guys and give them what they deserved. That was my sole motivation and it's served me well. But lately…"

"Lately what?"

"I'm seeing lots of gray areas out there. Not everything is cut and dried, black and white, like I thought. Not even killers."

"Meaning?"

"Sure, most murderers are just plain evil and it's a pleasure to nail them and bring them to justice. I've never doubted for a minute that it was my calling. But recently I've seen reasons behind some murders that change the way I feel. There are circumstances, although not totally justified, that at least make it understandable. There's people in that gray area. Lots of people. Barbara Atwell is one of them. I probably shouldn't say it out loud, but there's some garbage out there that might just deserve to die. It changes the way I see things, but I'm a cop first and you can count on me to do what's expected. Regardless.

"Don't ever lose sight of that, Reardon. Not for a minute. Those gray areas are up to judge or jury. Not you."

"Yes sir."

"Then we're done here. Now get to work. You've got a case to solve."

CHAPTER TEN

Doing the Crazy Cha-Cha

The two cops stood still as statues on the hot pavement of The Arizona Sonoran Desert Museum parking lot. Aaron Iverson was looking skyward and could smell the scent of rain that filled the pregnant clouds as they gathered and drifted over the distant mountains and toward the city of Tucson. Jerry Montana was focused on the tow drivers as they hitched the old green Chevy to the back of their truck with a heavy chain then drove away. But his thoughts were elsewhere. The last person he'd expected to hear from this morning was Detective Reardon. After the earful he'd given the Captain she should have been history. When he alluded to it, her response was curt and evasive. She knew what he was talking about so why was she still there? Were they going to let her wind up this case before they fired her? Why hadn't he been put in charge by now? Their first mistake was handing her a man's job that should've gone to a seasoned cop. It should have gone to him. They'd gotten it all backwards since day one and his resentment was growing like a flesh-eating bacteria and multiplying twice as fast.

But he'd finally gotten her. He just had to wait for the Captain to stop dragging his feet and act on it. About time that little trouble maker got her comeuppance. It had been worth the wait. And he'd caught her. She hadn't left that guys house until this morning. He'd seen her come and he'd seen her leave and he knew darn well it was someone she should have distanced herself from. She broke the rules. She was history. The respect he deserved was within reach now and it wouldn't be long before they'd all be calling him *Detective* Montana.

"Time to get to work," said Aaron, clapping his hands together and making Jerry nearly jump out of his skin. "Time to give the grounds one more scour."

"A thousand scrub brushes wouldn't make any difference. We've combed through every dirty inch of this place like rats in a garbage dump and there's nothing. I'm the one in charge here kid and I say screw it."

"But Maggie said…"

"You take your orders from me. Get in the car. We're going for a drive."

Jerry's mood was more foul than usual. Aaron could feel the hostility oozing from the cop's pours as they headed for the car. It made him uncomfortable and apprehensive, but this was the cop assigned to show him the ropes. Silently, he slid into the shotgun seat as Jerry got in behind the wheel and started the engine. He burned rubber as they sped across the parking lot and headed down the hill.

Aaron remained silent, white-knuckling it as the car sped towards the flats below, taking the dangerous curves like a roller coaster that had jumped its track and was in free fall. The man in charge of training him definitely had bugs gnawing at him, and Aaron just wanted to swat them and make them go away before they ended up flying off a cliff and into the saguaros. Jerry might not care if they ended up airborne but Aaron could think of a hundred better scenarios for the cause of his own demise.

Jerry didn't ease up on the gas pedal until they were nearing Silverbell Road, where he finally slowed down and stopped at the traffic signal. The light changed and they continued east toward the freeway. Jerry looked over to his right and spotted three young men standing outside a gas station, lost in conversation.

"Look," he said to Aaron, pointing in their direction. "They look like illegals, don't they?"

Aaron looked at the three of them, trying his best to make heads or tails of the comment. Jerry was acting crazier than a hungry Norsky at a lutefisk festival. There was no way, in Aaron's mind, that justified the accusation. They could just as easily be from families that had lived here since before Arizona became a state, yet Jerry had said it with such conviction that Aaron thought he might have seen neon signs around their necks. It made no sense. To him they were just three guys minding their own business and he wouldn't have given them a second glance.

"They look okay to me," he said.

"Then you've got a lot to learn. They're monsters. They fill their backpacks with drugs and crime and graffiti to poison our landscape. They're vermin. Nothing but rodents gnawing and gnawing and gnawing…"

It felt as if the bugs that had been eating away at Jerry had jumped ship and were now creeping along Aaron's flesh.

"Jeez Louise, Jerry. Isn't that a bit harsh?"

"You don't know what I know. Nobody does!"

"Yup, you betcha," he said, trying to appease him. "You're right Jerry. I've still got a lot to learn."

Things were going haywire right before Aaron's eyes and Jerry's radar was definitely malfunctioning. Minnesota was looking better and better to him with each passing second. He'd expected to run into some big city trouble, that's one of the reasons he'd come, but not trouble from a fellow cop. He had to diffuse this guy. He was definitely certifiable and increasingly out of control. Aaron spotted a coffee shop ahead and to their left.

"What do you say we stop for a cup of coffee?" he suggested, trying to distract him. The guy needed to calm down. And fast. "I could really use one. And maybe some pie to boot."

"Minny-sota apple pie? I'm not your mama and I ain't here to pamper you, Iverson. You should've stayed in the boonies where you belong."

Jerry jerked the wheel to the left and into oncoming traffic, nearly causing an accident as brakes squealed and a line of oncoming cars veered out of the way to avoid a collision. He wasn't headed for the coffee shop, he was headed back in the direction of the gas station.

He was looking for trouble and he was determined to find it, no matter how irrational.

"We're gonna check those guys out," he said. "Watch and maybe you'll learn something."

"It's probably nothing. C'mon, just let it be. Let's get that cup of coffee first, okay? Then we can see if they're still hanging around afterwards."

"Shut up, you stupid hayseed!"

Did this guy have even one likeable bone in his entire body?

They crossed traffic again as Jerry jumped the center line and into the gas station. He screeched to a halt and killed the engine. The three young men looked over, then casually turned their attention back to their conversation. One of them leaned against the building as the second one leisurely sucked his soda through a giant straw poked into an even larger paper cup. The third one laughed at something the first man had said.

Then all three of them broke into laughter.

"Did you see that?" Jerry asked.

"See what?"

"That guy laughed at us. No respect, no respect at all."

"I…"

"I think there's a drug deal going down, that's what I think. I can tell from here they're up to no good. Didn't the holy god of Hicksville give you eyes? If you can't spot trouble you'll never be a good cop. It's right in front of you. Can't you see it? You blind or something?"

"But…" Before Aaron could finish his sentence Jerry had bolted out of the car, his hand resting on his holster as he strutted arrogantly in the direction of the three young men. Aaron exited the car and hurried to catch up to him. The young men looked over, puzzled, as the two cops approached them, one of them strutting like Wyatt Earp at the O.K. Corral as the other tried to mask a look of utter panic.

"What are you up to?" Jerry demanded.

"We're just hanging out," one of them replied.

"Looks like more to me."

"We're not looking for trouble," said another, worry washing over his face.

"C'mon Jerry, let's just go," said Aaron, pulling on his sleeve. "This is a waste of time."

"Getting scum off the streets isn't a waste of time."

"They haven't done anything."

"If they haven't, then they were just about to. Weren't you boys?"

All three of them took a step backwards and exchanged glances.

"We're not doing anything but talking, just talking."

"You're loitering. Bet I'd find something if I searched you."

As his anger swelled, Jerry's voice climbed from bass to tenor to soprano and was quickly heading towards a high-pitched falsetto.

"You have no probable cause here, Jerry. Just cool it."

"You're out of your league and you don't know shit," he said, then gave one of them a shove that sent him reeling backwards. His friends caught him before he lost his balance.

"He's right," said the one he had shoved. "We're not doing anything but standing here minding our own business. Like he said, just cool it."

"Cool it? Cool it? How about you say cool it *sir?* You'd better start showing some respect."

A customer exited the store, glanced in their direction, then walked over to his car and left.

"Come on Jerry. Let's just go."

"We'll go when I'm good and ready to go and not a minute sooner. Don't you even think about telling me what to do! I'm not through with them yet. They're hiding something and I'm going to find out what it is."

Jerry was coming unglued and sounding more paranoid with each passing second.

"You want to search us, go ahead," one of them said softly, gesturing with his palms upward. "We've got nothing to hide. Nothing."

Montana's starting to scare the bejeebers out of these guys, Aaron thought. He could see it in their faces. They were trying to cooperate, to calm things down just as much as he was. Everybody was scared. Everybody except Montana, who was still itching for a confrontation and looking for any excuse to let loose.

But the young men continued to cooperate, which only served to amp up his level of frustration until he looked like he was going to burst and unleash all that bottled up hatred no matter what they did or didn't do. And God help the guy who was standing nearest to him when he blew.

"I'll search you when and if I damn well feel like it," he said. "I'm in charge here, not you punks. And not you either, Aaron 'you betcha' Iverson. That's what I call you behind your back, you know. You bloody *betcha* I do."

Things were starting to look like lose/lose all the way around.

One of them looked over at Aaron, a pleading expression on his face. Aaron wasn't sure what to do. He just wanted Montana to calm down and stop the craziness. Can you pull your gun on a fellow cop? How would he explain that? Would he even live to explain it? The way Montana was acting he was just as apt to take his poison out on him as the poor guys who were standing there shaking in their boots.

The sound of a ding-ding momentarily distracted Jerry Montana as a car pulled up to a pump and a middle aged woman got out. A flimsy straw hat covered her graying hair and she fished through her shoulder bag, took out her wallet and opened it. She pulled out a credit card and was posed to slide it into the slot and lift the hose. She looked over to where they were gathered and thought better of it. She got back into her car, restarted it and eased herself back into the traffic.

"Jerry. Jerry!" But Jerry wasn't listening, he was too busy giving the stink eye to the youths. Two of them turned away nervously as the third averted his glare and reached into his pocket.

"It's a gun!" Jerry yelled. "He's pulling a gun!"

The sunlight shimmered against metal as the man pulled the object from his pocket and raised it.

"Jerry, no!" Aaron yelled. "It's not a gun, it's a…"

The sound of gunfire muffled Aaron's words as him arm flew out and deflected Jerry's aim.

"It's a cell phone!" he finished. Jerry's gun fell to the ground at the same instant the young man fell against his friend, then melted down to the pavement.

There was blood.

"It was a friggin' cell phone for God's sake, what were you thinking?"

"He had a gun, I saw it, he drew a gun. He was aiming it at me, you saw it. You saw it. I was justified." A frozen Jerry just stood there mumbling his mantra as Aaron rushed over to where the young man lay, his two friends crouched over him.

"Awe geez," he said, looking at the guy. "Give me your t-shirt," he said to one of them. "Hurry!"

The man pulled off his t-shirt and handed it to the young cop, who grabbed it and pushed it against the shoulder wound to stave the bleeding. The other two rose and stood there, in shock, trying to make some sense out of what just went down.

"We weren't doin' nothing man, nothing."

"I know, I'm sorry, I know," was all Aaron Iverson could think to say. "I know, I'm sorry."

He looked over his shoulder and glared at Jerry Montana, who stood there doing nothing.

"Get on the radio!" he yelled to him. "Call for backup and call for an ambulance. Move!"

Montana's attention was focused on a place far away, a memory from a distant past. He snapped back at the sound of Aaron's voice and looked at the mayhem in front of him. How had it come to this, he wondered.

"There was a gun," he said, almost to himself, "I saw it."

"Go radio for help. Now!"

Jerry Montana turned, picked up his gun where it lay on the ground and walked slowly to the car. He was mumbling to himself as he opened the door and slid into the seat. He looked through the windshield at the small crowd gathering next to the building.

"We need backup out here," he said to the voice at the other end. "And we need an ambulance."

He watched the young cop leaning over and pressing his weight against the man's wound. At least the guy knew first aid if nothing else, he thought. But he ought to let the damn wetback bleed out. Serve him right. Serve them all right.

"I got them, Esperanza," he whispered to the shadow that haunted his mind. She was young and she was beautiful, just as he remembered her. "I finally got them."

Jerry looked again at the chaos as the rookie knelt above the bleeding youth. He glimpsed a shadow in the rear view mirror. The face that looked back at him wasn't his own. It was no longer the handsome young man who had lost the woman he loved. Instead the face was old and tired and wore a mask of exaggerated hatred and anger. It startled him when he realized who it was. Had his search for the monsters responsible for her murder turned him into a monster himself? Would Esperanza recognize him or would she recoil at what he had become? How could love create hatred, turn beauty into ugliness? When did it happen? He turned his face from the stranger in the mirror.

He'd had a moment of clarity and he didn't like what he saw.

The radio static called his name.

"Back up," he repeated. "An ambulance…and you'd better bring a body bag." And then as an afterthought he added: "And tell the Captain he can blame that damn Detective Maggie Reardon for this. It's all her fault."

He repeated the location, disconnected and watched the blur of activity through his windshield as if it were nothing more than a movie on a theater screen. He'd payed full price for the ticket and all he got in return was a second-rate movie with a "b-list" cast of players and a lame script. He deserved better than that. He'd earned it. He should have been the star. The hero.

"Is Jimmy gonna be okay?" one of the men asked Aaron.

"He'll be fine. It's only his shoulder, he'll be fine. Help is on the way."

"That cop nuts or what? We weren't doin' nothing, man. Nothing."

Aaron snapped his head around in the direction of a loud bang that came from somewhere behind him. He rose and handed the blood soaked cloth to the man who stood there shirtless and stunned and silent.

"Hold this onto his wound," he said, looking around for the source of the gun shot. He saw no one, but even at this distance he could see where it had landed. He wiped his bloody hands on his pants, unholstered his gun and raced to the squad car. As he neared the car, gun in hand, he spun around looking for an assailant. Again he saw no one. But he saw the pattern of blood spatter dripping down the inside of the windshield.

As he opened the car door he faced Jerry's lifeless body, his head leaning back against the headrest, his blood and gray matter morbidly decorating the interior. Then he saw the revolver in Jerry Montana's hand.

And the note gripped in the other.

Remember me as I was, it read. Nothing more.

There was a smile on crazy Jerry's dead face. He was grinning like he'd been looking at something real pretty, but what Aaron saw wasn't pretty at all. It was ugly.

And it was eerily sad.

He'd never seen a cop eat his gun before.

"Geez, Louise," he said and slammed the car door as he stifled his gag reflex. This was a mess in more ways than one, that was for darn sure.

He holstered his gun and walked away. A small crowd had gathered below the dark clouds that accumulated above their heads. The sun no longer shone as the first drops of rain mixed with the drying blood that dotted the pavement. The curious as well as a few would-be good Samaritans circled around the wounded man as his friend held tightly to him, telling him everything was going to be okay. Aaron walked in their direction, to the source of the escalating mayhem. Their building anger filled the air, mixing with the scent of wet creosote.

"You the cop that shot this kid?" Someone asked, pointing an accusatory finger at Aaron.

One of the three young men spoke up.

"He didn't do it," he said. "He was trying to help."

"Then what happened?"

"I don't know. The other cop just went totally postal on us. If it weren't for this one, it could've been a lot worse."

"Where's the cop with the trigger finger? Let me get my hands on him so I can tear him apart. Goddamn police brutality. I'll kill the sonofabitch." The guy was flexing his adrenaline muscles and ready to pounce.

"It's too late," said Aaron. "He's already dead."

"You save me the trouble?" The man sounded disappointed and faced the young cop who was calmly trying to diffuse his anger.

"He took care of that himself," said Aaron. "Now please step back and give us some breathing room."

Somewhere in the back of his mind he registered the sound of distant sirens as they came closer and closer.

CHAPTER ELEVEN

Murky Waters

Maggie stood to the side of the old green Chevy and watched the forensics tea, do their jobs. The worn paint-job was splattered with the morning rain. It had washed away desert dust as well as what might have been evidence. She felt like a chained dog, forbidden to tear into things until she got the signal. If she could have taken over every job in every department she would have. Things got done faster when you did them yourself. She hated the waiting game. But she had to step back and let the forensics experts comb through the old jalopy, gathering what they could.

"We ran the New Mexico plates," the man named George Timber-lake said. He walked over wearing a white lab coat, cotton gloves, and a slight limp that tilted him awkwardly to one side. "They came up stolen."

She sighed. "I need something."

"We lifted a few prints from the exterior. The rain took care of everything else. Man, the inside of that heap looks like a garbage dump. It's littered with empty cigarette packs, fast food containers, worn maps, old receipts, overflowing ashtray, you name it. All that junk's going to keep us busy for a long time. It looks like the guy might've been living in the old hoopty mobile. There's even a jar that looks like it's filled with urine. His own little port-a-potty. It smells something awful in there. Tidiness definitely wasn't one of John Doe's strong points. Good news is, we were able to pull a ton of prints from the inside. Joe's running them now."

No sooner had he spoken than Joe entered the garage and walked over to them.

"Looks like all those prints came from just two people. I checked with autopsy and one set belongs to our John Doe."

"No surprise there," said Maggie. "But it still doesn't tell us who he is."

"I ran them both through the system and came up with zilch. No criminal records on either of them. Whoever they belong to either kept their noses clean or were real good at flying below the radar."

"I think our vic wasn't so innocent. Somebody had it in for him. He had to have been up to some kind of no good," said Maggie.

"Or maybe he just witnessed something he shouldn't have."

"Wrong place, wrong time. That's a possibility. At this point anything's possible."

"I found something," one of them yelled over to them, holding up a small evidence bag with his gloved hand. George Timberlake limped over and took the clear plastic bag from his hand. He walked back to where Maggie stood, waving it above his head before she grabbed it from him. She held it up, looking at an old, worn Ohio driver's license, faded and curled up at its corners. Through the clear plastic bag she could see the I.D. photo. Her John Doe half-smiled back at her. And there was a name.

It was her first bingo moment.

"You know you can't take that yet," he said, taking it back from her.

"Could you at least xerox it for me?"

He sighed and walked away, returning a few minutes later to hand her a xeroxed copy of the drivers license.

"Thanks."

Shaking his head, George limped back to the car and opened the trunk.

"This guy's been busy," he said, looking at the scrap yard of license plates scattered throughout the interior. "There's plates in here from half the states in the union. And I'll bet my trick knee that every one of them was stolen. He was on the run from something." He spread them out face up and proceeded to photograph them before placing them in a large evidence bag.

"The evidence locker on this one is going to be packed tighter than Santa's toy bag on Christmas eve. We're going to be processing things for a long time," George said to her.

"Maybe there'll be a few presents in there for me."

"We've got a ton of trash to tag and bag, but take the driver's license copy and have at it".

She thanked him.

"I'd like photos of those plates before I go," she said. "Got a Polaroid?"

"You're an impatient one," he said. "Can't wait, huh?"

"Patience isn't one of my virtues."

George walked across the room and returned with an old camera. He dumped the bag of plates back into the trunk. His gloved hand lined the assortment of license plates face up. Maggie looked at the veritable map of the John Doe's travels as George snapped away, then handed her the photos as the camera slowly spat them out.

"Thanks, George," she said, then turned and left the men to their work.

When she reentered the main building total chaos slapped her across the face. Officers were running around the room while others huddled together, their words muffled and guarded. Tension filled the room. Phones rang, papers shuffled. From out the window she could see the press corps gathering like vultures, umbrellas held high protecting their perfect hair and their microphones and cameras from the rain. They elbowed each other for position, a hungry mob ready to pounce.

The Captain stood outside his office door, catching her attention with a wave of his hand. His face was ashen. His composure tenuous. She wove her way through the uniformed bodies and over to where he stood. He motioned her inside his office, slamming the door behind them.

"What's going on?"

"We've got a real problem, Reardon."

He sat down behind his desk, leaned forward in a defeated posture, and held his head in his hands.

"The press is gathering," she said, wondering why.

"They can stand out there until they're soaked to the skin for all I care. There will be no press conference until Jerry Montana's wife is informed. I'll be damned if she's going to hear it on the midday news."

Maggie took a seat across from him. "What did he do now?"

The Captain raised his head and spoke. He filled her in on the morning's events as best he could, barely stopping for a breath until he had finished.

Maggie was speechless.

"I guess this is your *I told you so* moment," he said.

"You know me better than that. I expected bad, but I never expected this bad."

"Either did I," he said. "Either did I. He left a note. All it said was 'remember me as I was.'"

"How considerate."

"I remember a good cop who let his grief poison him," he said in Montana's defense.

"The only thing anyone else is going to remember is a crazy cop who shot an innocent man before he blew out his own brains. The last thing he left wasn't a note. It was the toxic waste he spilled leaving the department to clean up the mess. That's his legacy."

"Point taken. The only good news is the victim is at St. Mary's and he's going to be okay. They got the bullet out of his shoulder, stitched him up, and he'll probably be released this afternoon. We've got someone over there getting statements from all three of them. Then we just wait for the negative headlines and the law suits."

"Were there any other witnesses?"

"Just to the aftermath. Except for Aaron Iverson."

"Where's Aaron? Is he alright?"

"He did a stand-up job all things considered. But we sent him straight to the department shrink. Everything else can wait. He was pretty shook up. He'll probably end up on administrative leave. At least until both he and the situation calm down."

"But he wasn't the shooter," she said.

"A gray area, but he was there."

Maggie thought long and hard before she spoke again.

"I could really use his help with my John Doe, Captain. Rather than putting him on ice, why not give him a desk job with me? It would keep him out of the field and still keep him useful."

"That call isn't yours and it isn't mine." He stood up. "Tell you what, Reardon. We'll see if the shrink thinks he can handle it, but don't get your hopes up. Right now I need somebody to go out and deliver the bad news to Jerry Montana's widow."

Maggie left the office before he had a chance to even think about assigning her the task. Telling somebody that the person they love is dead sucks worse than a domestic violence call. There are no right words to soften the blow. She went back to her desk and studied the xeroxed driver's license.

Delbert Frimel. John Doe. Delbert Frimel. Were she him she'd have chosen John Doe over his real name any day. She booted up the computer. How many Delbert Frimel's could be floating around out there? What had his parents been thinking when they looked at their newborn son and decided to stick him with a name like that? She doubted there were very many unfortunates stuck with that moniker.

She guessed one.

At least it should make the next step easier.

She pulled up the screen and typed in his name. Although his fingerprints had no hit in the system nor his dna in Codis she hoped that somehow the unusual name would.

Delbert Frimel.

There was a Jonas Frimel in South Dakota whose rap sheet was filled with nothing but a long list of petty thefts. And he was about twenty years too old.

She found a Lucille Frimel with a prostitution record in Vegas. Lucky Lucy. You go girl.

The last name that popped up was Frederick'Freddy' Frimel with some minor drug charges, but he was barely of legal age and by the looks of him he'd never see thirty.

And the address on his Ohio driver's license was non-existent.

Once again, she'd hit the old brick wall.

* * * *

He had planned on a chance meeting. That would have made the most sense. But she hadn't left her motel room and he was growing impatient. Being alone in the world was bad enough but she also had to be hungry. Hungry and alone. The last thing he wanted was for her to suffer any more than she already had.

He saw no alternative but to change his plan and find another approach to gain her trust.

An hour later someone knocked on her motel room door. One. Two. Three raps. Then silence. It couldn't be her husband, he'd have just used the key. And it couldn't be the front desk. They'd paid up a full week ahead and hung a sign on the door indicating no maid service. She'd rather use soiled towels than have some stranger snooping and poking around and making her edgy. It was one of the things he'd taught her as they traveled from motel to motel, from state to state. She muted the cartoon channel and slowly slid off the bed, not quite sure what to do.

Should she answer it?

It could be anybody.

It could be bad news.

She tiptoed over to the door and pressed her ear against it. No human sound came from the other side, not as much as a whisper. Just the relentless, pounding rain. She pressed her eye against the peep hole. No face stared back at her. She stepped to the window at her left and pulled back the curtain, ever so slightly.

She looked to the left and to the right and saw no one.

After working up her courage, she slipped off the chain lock and loosened the deadbolt.

Just one step.

One rule broken.

One step couldn't hurt.

She opened the door just enough to take that one brave step. Her bare foot bumped against something. A large paper bag encased in a larger plastic bag to protect it from the rain sat at her feet. She looked around and thought she glimpsed the back of a man as he slipped into a room down the hallway. Or maybe it was just a shadow in the rain playing tricks with her vision. Or it could have been nothing at all.

Strange, she thought.

The mystery bag intrigued her. She lifted it. It was heavy. She stepped back into the room, flipped the deadlock and re-slid the protective chain back into place.

The aroma hinted at its contents.

Food.

Someone knew she was hungry. Were there really such things as guardian angels? She sat in the middle of the bed, turned the sound back on the television and opened the bag. She removed the first item. A large bag of iced animal crackers. They'd always been her favorites. White ones and pink ones, covered with round sprinkles. She'd always eaten the pink ones first, saving the white ones for last because they tasted best. How could the angel have known how much she liked them, or did guardian angels know everything? She found the idea of someone knowing things about her unnerving. Even if it was an angel. Were there dark angels? She'd been taught to always be on alert, to always be suspicious. He said it had served them well. Her hand reached into the bag and began pulling out the items one by one and tossing them onto the bedspread. There was a chunk of cheese with a plastic knife carefully tapes to its wrapping. A box of crackers. A quart of milk and a plastic bowl and spoon. A big box of breakfast cereal. It didn't have a cartoon face on it, but it was welcome just the same. There were two fresh apples and an orange. The item at the bottom of the bag was wrapped in layers of tissue paper and it was warm to the touch. She pulled it out and unwrapped it, lifting the edge of the top bread slice and exposing layers of warm roast beef slathered in mayonnaise. She ate it in record time as the voice of Woody Woodpecker laughed from the television.

Between bites she laughed along with him.

When finished, she rose from the bed and carefully lined up the remaining food along the length of the dresser. She'd make it last, however long that might be.

She leaned across the bed, balled up the sandwich wrapper to shove it into the large paper bag. Something caught her eye. A small piece of paper looked up at her from its bottom. A receipt? She pulled it out, unwrinkled it and smoothed it out. Scrawled across it were three words: *Don't be afraid.*

But she was afraid.

Was this gift of food some kind of lure, like a crumb in a mousetrap waiting for her to take the bait? Well, she'd taken it. She was hungry and now she wasn't hungry any more. If it had been a trap it had succeeded.

Did guardian angels leave notes? Or was it an ogre who wanted to feed her, just to fatten her up so he could then eat her himself? Had he eaten her husband and was now coming for her?

She walked across the room and lay the note next to the stash of food.

Her heart raced as sat down on the bed. She flipped through the channels on the television, then turned it off. She needed quiet so she could think.

She reached for the phone, but all the instructions taped to it confused her. There were so many numbers. She studied it. She debated her next move.

It was up to her.

"Okay," she finally said. "All I have to do is hit '9' for an outside number.

Her fingers hit the number, waited for the dial tone, then punched in '911' and waited.

A voice picked up at the other end.

What would she say? That someone left her food? That would sound crazy. Would she tell them her husband was missing? That she was alone and scared? Was the voice at the other end nothing more than another trap?

She slammed it back onto its cradle and started to cry.

If only he was here to tell her what to do.

CHAPTER TWELVE

The Guardians

It was evening and the sky was still crying, washing its ocean of tears into the arroyos and gutters of Tucson. An occasional flash of lightning lit up the sky, accompanied by the reverberation of thunder. Intermittent gusts of wind slammed the rain against shuddering window panes. The year's first rains had already done their job. Plants that had withered plumped and came to life. Water was the lifeblood of the desert and wild flowers had blossomed their thanks, adding an array of color to the sepia landscape. Their party dresses of yellows and oranges and purples covered the browns and tans and ochers of the parched ground and hillsides. This second rain washed dust from the saguaros and streets and tile rooftops. It trapped cars in flash floods and blocked roads and created more potholes. It puddled itself into every indentation and depression it could find to provide drink for the wildlife as well as breeding grounds for the mosquitos, plump with eggs.

And it erased evidence from an old, green Chevy.

Detective Maggie Reardon was packing it in for the day. She filed away papers and turned off the stubborn computer that had refused to give her answers. She stood, grabbed her bag and took a step towards the exit. She wanted to get to her car and light up a smoke. The ringing cell phone stopped her in her tracks. She was tempted to keep walking. Her day was done. But it kept ringing. She pulled it out of her purse and answered.

"Detective Reardon."

"You could at least have given me a heads up," said the voice at the other end.

It was a man's voice. It was Rocco La Crosse.

What was he talking about?

"Maggie, are you there?"

"I'm here."

"Why didn't you tell me Barbara was released? She called me from jail. She was being let go and needed a ride home."

Rocco was in a snit and Maggie was embarrassed.

She'd forgotten about him. And Barbara. A dead cop can be a distraction.

"Rocco, I forgot."

"She's free and that wasn't important enough for a simple call? Good God, Maggie."

Maggie reached into her bag and pulled out her Camels, slid a cigarette out and pressed it between two fingers. It posed there, impatiently waiting for a flame. She put the unlit cigarette in her mouth and inhaled on it, a pacifier while she tried to form the right words. She didn't need Rocco's anger to top the pile of crap the day had already dumped on her.

"Calm down and listen," she said. "All hell broke loose here. In the confusion it slipped my mind."

"Why didn't you call?"

She took another drag from her unlit cigarette, pretending her lungs were filling with its lovely poison instead of the squad room's stale air. She didn't have the energy or inclination to play twenty questions.

"I'm fried and I don't have time for this. Turn on the news."

She disconnected him.

Then regretted it.

It was unfair to dump her frustration on him.

Within five minutes the phone rang again.

It was Rocco.

"Okay, I watched the news and it wasn't good."

"I shouldn't have hung up."

He ignored her half-apology.

"We can see each other now, right? Come over to Barbara's and help us empty these wine bottles. Sounds like you could use it."

"I want to go home, pour some Irish and call it a day."

"Understood. I get you, Maggie Reardon. I know where I stand on your priority list."

"So why bother?"

"I'm a masochist," he said. "Put that in my plus column."

"You're crazy, Rocco."

"Why else would I put up with you?"

"The only reason that makes sense, you unfortunate. Tell Barbara I'm happy for her. And I'm curious about something. How did your lawyer manage to get the attorney to drop the charges?"

"Let's just say that if his wife knew what he was up to, his cash cow would divorce him, and quickly."

"It'd serve him right, I'm sure. I've never liked the man. He doesn't walk, he struts. He's arrogant. But whatever he's hiding he's doing a good job of it."

"If it ever surfaces he'll lose a lot more than his wealthy wife. Listen, Maggie. I need to say this. You and I both have lives that are separate from the *us*. That's healthy."

"I don't need or want somebody who sucks up all my oxygen."

"Breathing space. There's nothing sadder than couples glued together at the hip. They create a dual identity and the individuals vanish. Every sentence starts with *we* rather than *I*."

"We're more alike than I thought."

Her sigh of relief whispered through the phone and into Rocco's ear. He got it.

"How about tomorrow night for that Italian dinner?"

"Your place? Even artists and cops have to eat. I'm game if you are."

"The game of what makes Maggie tick?"

"Good luck, I haven't figured myself out yet."

"Wait, before you haaaang up…" his words had begun to slur. He'd already started on her share of that wine. "We've been working our butts off on the next show. We'll be celebrating a few new artists and Barb's return. A real gala of thanks. Will you come?"

"I wouldn't miss it."

Maggie saw Aaron Iverson dragging himself into the squad room.

"Gotta go now," she said.

"I'll fill you in tomorrow."

She hung up and looked over at Aaron. His lily white skin sagged, accentuated by the dark circles under his tired, bloodshot eyes. Today had to be number one on his bad day list.

"Maggie, I'm glad you're still here."

She rose from her chair and walked over to where he was leaning against a wall.

The poor guy looked lost. They stood in awkward silence. The cop in her battled with her emotions. The cop lost. A death cut to the bone, unlike a skinned knee you could kiss and make better. The Captain's words replayed in her head. *Don't go getting all touchy-feely on me.* But he wasn't here. A hug could be downright therapeutic and the kid looked like he needed one. It lowers the blood pressure. They were cops, sure, but that didn't mean they weren't human. So she played mama bear and hugged him. Not a good idea after all. It felt awkward.

"Dumb of me," she said, "but…"

"My mom says a hug's better than a bunch of words any day."

Slightly embarrassed, she quickly changed the subject.

"How are you holding up?"

"I'm handling it."

"A pretty nasty initiation into the dirty underbelly of police work."

"Yup. Don't get much of that back home. Just bar fights, mostly. People like their beer and pretzels. Keeps us warm during cold winters, then kinda spills into the rest of the year."

"Here the excuse is keeping cool in the summer heat."

"People are people, even in the boondocks. We had a bank president who siphoned off some money. It shocked and hurt some folks but at least there was no blood."

And Aaron's day had leaked enough blood to fill a beer stein.

"How'd the obligatory visit with the shrink go?"

He shrugged.

"Thanks for keeping your promise," he said.

"My promise?"

"About working with you. Between me, the Captain and the shrink I got the thumbs up, but I have to see her more. Just routine. They're keeping me off the street. And away from the press. But they're letting me assist you."

"I wish it were under better circumstances."

"If it weren't for you I'd have high-tailed it out of here and never looked back."

"You handled things as well as any seasoned cop on the force."

"My baptism by fire. You knew Jerry Montana was wrong in the head, didn't you?"

"He was ten scoops of crazy on steroids."

"I sensed he wasn't right, but all I feel is sad. He didn't have to go and do that."

"Shooting that guy or himself?"

"Both, but mostly what he did to himself. Suicide's a damn permanent solution to a temporary problem."

"He'd have thought it through. Best case scenario, psych leave. Or turning in his badge. At worst he'd end up behind bars. In general population he'd get shived by an inmate faster than a pedophile."

"Limited menu options."

Maggie thought about the cops who'd eaten their guns. There were plenty. They had their reasons. Dealing with the dark side was depressing. There are images that etch themselves into your head and never go away. Murders, abused kids, domestic violence, overdoses. You name it. Unlike the sanitized stories one scans in the newspapers or watches on tv, a cop sees it up close and personal. The smell of death can numb your ability to step out from the shadows, to see that the sun still rises. The malignancy could wind around you so tight you couldn't breathe. And there were career cops, who once they were retired, lost their identity. They were their badge and they didn't know how to be anything else. Their gun was their friend, the bullet their solution. It beat rotting away as a night watchman. And then there was Jerry. He got rid of his demons with a pull of the trigger, and avoided paying the piper his due.

He was probably right.

She had no uplifting words for the rookie who stood before her. There were none.

"Are you up to starting first thing in the morning? I've got some research you can sink your teeth into. Our John Doe is a real mystery man."

"I'll be ready."

"Tomorrow then."

Maggie headed out the door, ran through the rain to her car, got in and slammed the door. Before she shoved the key into the ignition she tried to light her rain soaked cigarette. She swore at it, threw it into the ashtray and pulled a dry one from the pack. She lit it, leaned back and inhaled deeply. It was almost as relaxing as that bottle of whiskey waiting for her at home.

* * * *

The storm refused to subside. The more seasoned travelers exited the freeway off-ramps seeking cover. Tucson was the last big stop for those heading north to Phoenix or the Grand Canyon, the last major town for those brave enough to head for the border to the south. Tucson's motels and hotels quickly filled with those smart enough not to challenge heavy rains. The only time they were this busy was when the Gem and Mineral Show hit town. Vendors and buyers crossed state borders or descended from the skies, weary from long flights.

It was one week when Tucson raked in the big bucks.

Tonight the Pink Flamingo Motel on Miracle Mile filled to capacity, its parking lot full. The crumbling facade shadowed the nineteen-fifties, a decade when it was fresh and new and welcomed tourists with ironed cotton shirts and Bermuda shorts. A time when it was a destination rather than a stop-over. Now it barely managed to stay above water, depending on a clientele with enough pocket money for a single night's stay. Or someone needing a bed for an hour, no questions asked.

The Flamingo was two steps up from flop-house or falling victim to the bulldozer. It held on like a fading movie star holds onto yesterday's memories, long after beauty fades. The broken neon sign flickered in the dark, a reminder that a thick coat of make-up can hide only so much.

Behind the door to room twelve, the young woman tossed and turned, unable to sleep. He hadn't yet returned. She wondered where he was. And when he would come back. Or if he ever would. Making decisions had always been his job, not hers. Would he want her to make one now or just wait? Her mind played over decisions and consequences and added to her confusion. Several times she'd worked up the courage to call 911, but she hung up every time she heard the voice at the other end. At three in the morning she hung up for the last time and drifted into an uneasy sleep.

* * * *

An hour later the phone rang, waking her.

No one knew she was there.

She could let it ring.

She could answer it.

Either decision could be the wrong one.

Her arm reached across the bed and picked up. It was the 911 operator. How could he have known that she was the caller? How could he have known where the call had come from? It frightened her but she fought to keep her voice calm. He said he wanted to be sure there was no problem. He asked if she could speak freely. He told her that if she was in danger to just say it was a wrong number and hang up and he'd send help. She had to think. Fast. The last thing she wanted was the mysterious gestapo coming for her.

"No, I'm okay," she finally said. "It was a mistake."

He didn't sound convinced.

"It was my little boy. You know how kids can be. He kept playing with the phone. It was an accident. I'm sorry I bothered you." It surprised her that lying had come so easily.

She listened, then did her best to reassure him.

"I told him it was a bad thing to do. He's asleep now. It won't happen again."

Her hands shook when she hung up.

Her heart thumped like a trapped rabbit.

Sleep was impossible.

With a trembling hand she picked up the remote and turned on the television so she wouldn't be alone. She kept the volume low so as not to disturb anyone in the adjacent rooms. She watched the weather channel and waited for the darkness to ease its way into daylight.

Morning came, the rain stopped, the television droned.

She sat upright on the sagging mattress, frozen in a holding pattern of indecision.

The only motion she could manage was to switch from the weather channel to the early morning cartoons.

CHAPTER THIRTEEN

Room Twelve

"Good morning, Miss Maggie," said Carlos when she came through the door. He lowered his head and stared at the cash register to avoid eye contact.

"You're here," she said. His nephew was gone and her friend was back. She was relieved to see him where he belonged. Right where he'd been standing for as long as she could remember.

"You really had me scared, Carlos. I thought something happened to you."

"But Ramon said to you that I was fine. Just as I told him to."

Carlos kept his head down, brown eyes peering up at her like a guilty child.

"But Carlos, I was worried."

"I did not mean to worry you. But I have a surprise," he said, his hand covering his mouth as he spoke.

"A good one, I hope. I'm could use a shot of good news."

"*Si,* very good news."

He removed his hand from in front of his mouth and held his chin high, wearing a big Cheshire cat grin. His discolored teeth were gone, replaced with white ones that shone in bright contrast to his dark complexion. He'd probably gone to one of those discount places, she thought, the kind that fixes you up with new choppers in a day. But they were pearly white, just as the commercials promised. Bargain basement or not, they'd done a great job. He stood taller and looked twenty years younger.

"What do you think, Miss Maggie?"

"I think you're one handsome devil."

"I thank Ramon. He is a good man."

"He seems nice."

"He is, although this was not always so. When he was younger he went *loco* and turned to the gangs. I talked to him like a father.'No good can come from this,' I told him. Think beyond actions. Think of consequences.' I told him God gave him a brain and he should use it. 'You have family,' I said. 'Is your gift to them going to be an invitation to your funeral before you are twenty?'"

"Or life in a wheelchair with a bullet lodged in his spine," she said. "Not the kind of wheels teenagers visualize for themselves."

"He had never seen me so angry. It surprised him and he listened to his Uncle Carlos. He now has an honest job and I am proud. But recently he spoke to me like I used to speak to him. He told me my life should be more than this store, that I needed to be good to myself."

He proudly flashed another smile, showing off his new teeth. "This is good, *si*?"

"This is good," she said. "Antonio Banderas has got nothing on you. Now you need an excuse to show them off."

"I smile for my customers."

"Like Ramon said, the store shouldn't be your life."

"Like your job is to you?"

"I'm working on that."

"And you have seen your new, young gentleman?"

Maggie could tell that her expression told him everything.

"Ah, I see," he said with a wink.

"Let's just say that he's putting up with me. So far."

Customers were filing into the store so Maggie filled her coffee cup, paid her friend and left. Tucson flew past her windshield as she headed for work. She drove past empty lots filled with weeds. Small *casitas* and new structures with well-manicured yards stood side by side. Shining high-rises loomed above small storefronts and brightly painted *bodegas*. The town was a patchwork of the old and new, stitched side by side like a poorly thought out crazy quilt.

The rain had stopped. The morning sun was working overtime to bake away what moisture hadn't already sucked deep into the dry, hungry ground or run off into the gutters. The endless circle would continue and soon people would again be praying for the rain instead of cursing it.

* * * *

Maggie had a work space set up next to her own desk so that Aaron Iverson could get down to business. He settled into the chair next to her and turned on the computer, impatiently waiting for it to boot up so that he could get to work. He needed a distraction from the dark cloud that hovered over the room. Usually astir with activity and conversation it was eerily silent in the aftermath of yesterday's events.

Her desk phone rang. She answered it.

"Interesting," she said. "An imaginative cause of death to say the least."

A few more words were exchanged before she hung up.

"They've got the cause of death on our guy," she said to Aaron. "The weapon might have been a philips screwdriver. Maybe an ice pick or something similar. Whatever was used it was

narrow and sharp and the damage wasn't easy to detect. It was jammed through his ear canal and into his brain."

"Maximum results with minimal blood."

"You any good with computers?"

"Easy-peasy. I'm as good as any pimple-faced geek out there."

Maggie handed him the copy of the worn out driver's license.

"Our John Doe has a name. Delbert Frimel. I ran him through CO-DIS, ran his prints, ran his name through the system. Nothing. Why don't you play around and see if you can find a hit? There's got to be something on him somewhere."

Delbert Frimel was living rent-free inside Maggie's head and she wanted to evict him as soon as possible. If they could find something on the who, maybe they could figure out the why. And the why might give them the lead they needed to make some kind of connection.

Somebody out there had a reason for wanting him dead.

"While you're working on that," she continued, "I'm going to take one final look-around out at the museum grounds. It's been gone over thoroughly so odds are the weapon walked out with the perp, but I'll give it another once over before I okay taking down the tape."

"That ought to make the Museum happy," he said.

"Later," she said as she rose and headed for the door. The officer working the front desk motioned her over. Like most of the other cops wandering around this morning, he didn't look as if he'd had much sleep. Thinking about a dead fellow officer can do that. You start to think about yourself, how you're just one pull of the trigger away from sharing his hole in the dirt.

"911 got a series of calls last night," he began. "Several hang-ups from the same number. The operator called back and was told everything was fine. But something about it doesn't sit right. The caller said her kid had been playing with the phone, but who's kid is up at 3:30 in the morning?"

"Could be something. Could be nothing at all."

"Would you swing by there when you find time?"

He handed her a piece of paper scrawled with the name and address of The Pink Flamingo Motel on Oracle Road.

"The 911's came from Room Twelve," he said. "Maybe it's because this wouldn't be the first time somebody took a permanent slumber on one of their mattresses, but something about those calls doesn't smell right."

"If the world smelled like fresh-baked cookies we'd be out of work." She shoved the paper into her pocket and headed for the exit.

* * * *

"Go away!" she yelled through the motel room door. "Just go away."

"I need to talk to you."

Knock. Knock. Knock.

"No."

Knock. Knock.

"I'm a friend."

Knock.

"No, you're a stranger."

One blue eye peered out the keyhole only to see another blue eye staring back.

Could he see her too?

She placed her hand over the keyhole and took a step backwards.

It was unnerving.

The knocking stopped.

"A stranger? No, a friend." The voice said.

"You speak in tongues. Go away or I'll call the front desk."

"Think on it," the young man said. "I can wait. I'm good at waiting, but I'll be back."

She didn't want him to come back. Despite his kindness in leaving her food, maybe because of it, he frightened her. Why should anyone care about her? How could he have known she was in trouble? Did he know her husband was missing? And if so, how and why? And why should it matter?

She turned back into the room, listening as his footfalls faded farther and farther away until she could no longer hear them. She didn't exhale until she heard a door close down the hall. The possibilities spun around in her head, making her dizzy. Making it impossible to relax.

The only thing she knew for sure was what her husband told her. Everyone is a stranger. Strangers are danger. Never trust anyone.

* * * *

Maggie spent an hour walking the grounds at the Arizona-Sonoran Desert Museum. At least now she had a better idea what she was looking for. It wasn't a gun. It wasn't a knife. She looked under cacti, kicked her feet through the dirt that skirted the pathways, looked beneath the foliage of the sturdy and strange desert plants. There was no sense checking the trash cans and bins. They'd been sifted through and nothing resembling a weapon had been found. Whatever had been used for the kill had definitely walked out through the front gate with the person who'd left that body behind like yesterday's garbage.

The sun was climbing higher in the cloudless sky. She was wasting time and was ready to move on to the next step of the investigation. Hopefully Aaron Iverson had come up with something on Delbert Frimel. There had to be a record of him. Nobody went through this world without leaving a footprint somewhere.

Something more than a beat up driver's license.

She pulled out her cell and called headquarters.

"You can send someone out to AZDM to pull down the tape," she said. "I'm heading over to Oracle Road. No, it was probably nothing but a liquor-soaked spat, but who knows? Sometimes they fight 'til they pass out, but sometimes it escalates. Hopefully it was the former."

Maggie hiked back to the front entrance. The same grouchy woman was sitting behind the glass at the ticket window staring into space with nothing to do but tell people they were closed. Apparently not everyone had heard. Some people came from out of town. Some people lived in a bubble.

The woman jumped when she tapped on the glass and told her to spread the word that they could once again open for business. Their big shot had been hounding them and Maggie was in no mood. Grumpy could have the pleasure of relaying the news.

And the Captain would be relieved to have him off his back.

She exited and walked across the parking lot.

The car seat was a hot plate, the interior even hotter. She revved the engine, rolled down the window and turned the air conditioner full blast to blow out the heat. She pulled a cigarette from it's pack and cupped it in her hand so she could light it. It was amazing how anything so bad could taste so good. It was her guilty pleasure, like a fat person savoring a banana split and telling himself it had no calories if no one was watching.

Sliding into drive, she headed out and smoked her way towards town. She ground out the stubble in the ashtray and turned on the radio to an oldies station. Julie London was singing Cry Me A River. One of her father's favorites. Julie's sad, smoky voice whispered its soulful lament, blending with the zephyr of cold air blowing through the air conditioning vents.

Maggie daydreamed her way to Oracle Road.

* * * *

The young man's determination had paid off, but his patience was gone. He couldn't help himself. It was time for the next step. Once again he stood outside the door to room twelve, knocking.

No one answered.

Not even a voice telling him to go away.

He'd try again later.

Maggie Reardon sat in her car in the parking lot of The Pink Flamingo Motel, watching. She watched as the man turned and walked away and entered his room two doors down. No one had opened the door when he'd knocked. Maybe the woman who'd made the emergency calls had already checked out. Maybe he'd been a customer from the previous night looking for a mid-day encore before hitting the road.

Turning a trick was as common as working in a fast-food joint and didn't pay much better.

She unhooked her seatbelt and exited the car.

When she knocked no one answered, but she could hear the soft murmur of the television. She knocked again.

"I said to go away," said a female voice.

"Tucson police," Maggie said. "Open up."

A shadow crossed the peep hole.

"Just a few questions, ma'am." She smiled, imagining that's how Jack Webb would've said it back when he wore Badge 714.

The lock clicked, the chain slid, the door opened a crack.

"I haven't done anything."

"Just a follow-up on your 911 calls. Can we talk?"

"Do I have a choice?"

"Life's full of choices. Consider me an easy one."

Hesitantly, she opened the door and let her in.

"I'm sorry to interrupt," said Maggie. The girl wore no make-up to cover her pale features and her long prairie skirt made her look more like a Utah child-bride than a hooker. She didn't have to be holding a Book of Mormon for Maggie to guess she wasn't a working girl. She was alone, but noticed a few men's shirts hung between them and the bathroom. No indication of a child; the one who supposedly dialed 911 several times by accident, beating the odds of winning the lottery.

"Your name?"

The question caught the woman off guard. She looked up at the popcorn ceiling as if it held the answer to the simplest of questions.

"Mary," she finally said. "Mary Smith."

"Detective Maggie Reardon."

The best she could come up with was Mary Smith? If she was lying she was no pro, not by a long shot. And her husband's name was probably John. Yea, right. John and Mary Smith from Anytown, U.S.A.

"About those calls…"

"It was a mistake. I told the operator I was sorry."

"Are you here with someone?" Maggie asked, indicating the shirts.

"My husband is out working," she said, toying with the cheap wedding band on her finger.

Maggie saw no bruises or scratches on her, but some men are good at doing damage where it doesn't show.

"Did you have a fight?"

"No. Nothing like that. We never fight. Never."

"You can tell me."

"He's a good man."

So the husband takes off for work and the man down the hall comes knocking? She didn't seem the type, but looks can be deceiving. Something about her wasn't right, but she couldn't put her finger on it. Maybe it was just that she seemed so child-like, so unsure of every word. Maggie looked over at the television, at the cartoons. Embarrassed, the woman picked up the remote and turned it off.

"Where's your child?"

"My child?"

"The one that made the phone calls."

The woman wore that familiar deer in the headlights look. One simple question, yet she had to think before answering. Maggie waited. And wondered why the hesitant woman was so guarded in her words as well as her actions. Every move she made was thought out. Every word carefully chosen.

The cop back at the desk had a good nose. Most cops did. She was hiding something. But everybody was hiding something. Big things, little things, it didn't matter. We all hide something we fear would make the world think less of us. Or make us think less of ourselves.

"Oh," she finally said. "That 911 person must've misunderstood me. It wasn't my child. I was babysitting."

"Babysitting?"

"A little boy. For a couple on the second floor. I figured why not make a few dollars, you know?"

Maggie wondered if she'd picked up some spare cash from the guy down the hall too, but it just didn't fit. Being odd didn't make her a criminal.

"And you babysat all night?"

Another long pause.

"They went partying or something."

"Their names? Their room number?"

The young woman stared down at the dingy carpet, flicking cereal crumbs with her bare toes.

"They picked him up first thing this morning. They checked out."

No way to back up her convenient answer. Maggie was getting nowhere fast, so she wrote her off as a waste of time. Just one more person who couldn't figure out 911 was for *real* emergencies and not for complaining that McDonald's forgot their slice of pickle. If that was a crisis how did the idiots handle a real problem?

"That's it then. How long will you be staying?"

"Why?"

"In case I have more questions."

The young woman shrugged her shoulders. She wanted the cop to go away. And stay away. She didn't like questions. Lying was hard. Why all the fuss over a stupid 911 call? Making those calls was dumb and now she had this cop snooping into her business.

"Why did you come?"

"To make sure you were alright."

"I'm fine. Everything's fine. Again, I'm sorry for your...inconvenience." There, that sounded good. Inconvenience was a big word.

"How long did you say you'd be here?"

If she'd been brave enough to go through the door alone, she'd have been gone. But he'd be upset if he came back and she wasn't there. She had to wait for him.

"Your guess is as good as mine," she said.

It was barely perceptible, but when Maggie placed her business card in the woman's hand she noticed a slight tremble. The woman quickly covered that hand with her other one.

"My number's on there should you need me," Maggie said and left. She had more important items on her menu, none of them appetizing.

Aaron Iverson would have said she had bigger fish to fry.

Hopefully he'd come up with an ingredient or two so they could stir up some Delbert Frimel.

It was time to pull out the pan and start cooking.

CHAPTER FOURTEEN

Highways and Headstones

"I got a hit on that Frimel guy," Aaron Iverson called out when he saw Maggie Reardon enter the room. He was sitting at the computer with a big, mid-western grin washing across his face. "Delbert Frimel has an address and it's not the vacant lot he had listed on his Ohio driver's license."

Maggie walked over and leaned against his desk.

"What've you got?" she asked. "Where's his home base?"

"I've been going around and around with that name and finally found something," he said proudly. "I even went on Ancestry.com and started searching birth and death certificates. The guy had to be somewhere."

"Cut to the chase, Iverson."

"Okay, okay. You're an impatient one, anybody ever tell you that?"

A thousand times, Maggie thought. It was a comment that signaled Aaron was entering the comfort zone. It was better than having him tiptoeing on eggshells, worrying about saying the wrong thing or making the wrong move. He was finally right where he needed to be.

"No argument on that," she said, unoffended. "Patience isn't one of my virtues. Now give me the skinny on Frimel."

Aaron cleared his throat.

"He resides in Sunbury, Pennsylvania."

"The address?"

"Get this," he said. "He's sleeping peacefully in a plot at Holy Cross Cemetery."

"Son of a…"

"Now it gets interesting. Our mystery man got his driver's license a couple months after the real Delbert Frimel got covered with his dirt blanket back in Pennsylvania. I.D. theft. He probably just read the obits or walked through a couple of graveyards."

"All you need is a copy of a dead person's birth certificate. Some-body close to your own age. It's easy. And even easier to get a driver's license from that. Then you've got a nice, new identity with your photo to prove it."

"Easy peasy. But it makes me wonder why he didn't use those ID's to get a passport and skip the country."

"It depends what he was running from. It could've been anything from petty theft to murder to anything in between."

"Or maybe he wasn't smart enough to think that far ahead."

Aaron and Maggie bounced their ideas back and forth like ping-pong balls.

"If he was stealing plates he was probably stealing cars."

"If he was smart he lifted plates from cars other than the ones he stole. Old cars. Cops might keep on the lookout for recent models. They're worth more. The owners would complain more. But older cars wouldn't be worth the bother. If an officer stumbled across one fine, if not then no big loss."

"Right. And he kept heading west. His target might have been Mexico."

Aaron laughed. "Here in Arizona I'll bet you don't get many people sneaking across the border *into* Mexico."

Maggie sat down and shuffled through the mess on her desk. She picked up the Polaroid photo of the license plates she'd gotten from forensics and studied it. A trunk full of tin, in no particular order stared back at her. She picked up the phone and called down to the evidence room.

"Detective Reardon here. You got the evidence in yet from the murder out at the Desert Museum? Great. I'm sending down Aaron Iverson."

She hung up.

"Aaron, get downstairs and pull the box on this. There should be a big bag of license plates in the evidence locker. Bring those up here asap. We've got some traveling to do."

Aaron took off and Maggie pulled up a map of the United States on her computer.

He returned in record time, the large bag of license plates in hand.

"Clear your desk. Push it up against mine," she said, clearing off her own desk. "We need some room to spread these out."

The sound was like the metal on metal screech of a train coming to a halt as he pushed his desk the few inches across the floor. He lined it up against hers, then dumped out the plates.

They counted seven.

"Okay," she said. "The phony driver's license was from Ohio, Delbert Frimel croaked in Pennsylvania. Let's put some order to these." She looked up at the United States map on her computer screen.

"Is there a plate from Ohio or Pennsylvania?"

"Both," he said, handing them to her.

She placed the Pennsylvania plate on the left corner of his desk. "This was the starting point," she said. "Logic says Ohio was step two."

"He was running from something, or someone, and was good at erasing himself."

Maggie hit the print key and the printer spat out the map. She rose from her chair and retrieved it, slapping it down on her desk. "This'll make it easier," she said, circling Sunbury, Pennsylvania with a black, felt tipped marker.

"Where in Ohio was the driver's license issued?"

"Springfield."

Maggie grabbed the Ohio license plate and placed it next to the one from Pennsylvania. "Step two," she said. "What are the other states?"

Aaron shuffled through them. "New Mexico, Illinois, Oklahoma, Missouri. This guy sure made tracks. Oh, and Arkansas."

"I'd bet there was a trail of stolen cars that followed the same path," Maggie mumbled to herself as she studied the map. "Put Illinois next to Ohio. Put Missouri after that. Now Arkansas."

She circled the states as Aaron lined up the license plates.

"Oklahoma next."

"That leaves New Mexico as the caboose," he said, placing it at the end of the line. "Oh, I checked it out and the Delbert Frimel driver's license was first issued ten years ago, so it must've been close to that time that our guy hit the road and took on his new identity."

"Ten years is a long time to be on the lam," she said as she circled New Mexico. "A person can do six, maybe seven-hundred miles a day. Eight-hundred max, but that'd be pushing it. This guy settled awhile in several places…"

"He'd have needed money to keep on the move."

"If Frimel was that hard to get a hit on he worked menial labor along the way."

"Getting paid under the table. No record. No trail."

"Dishwashing. Bussing tables. Day labor."

She studied the map, running her fingers along the routes Delbert Frimel/John Doe might have driven. Instead of taking major arteries he likely kept to minor, less traveled roads. It would take longer but there was less chance of being spotted.

"No, Pennsylvania isn't step one," she corrected. "It's step two. Step one, the location from where he started, would have been east of there. He'd have been on the road awhile before hitting Pennsylvania." Her marker traced an outline of the United States from New York and all the way north to Maine. New York, Connecticut, Massachusetts, Vermont, New Hampshire and Maine. One of those states had to have been his starting point. If he was on the run there was no way he'd have started in New Jersey or Maryland and headed north before veering to the west. He's have looked for the fastest way to get the hell out of Dodge.

That narrowed the number of search states to six, eliminating a whopping forty-four.

"I've got another project," she said, handing him the map. "Go back ten years on each of these states and bring up what crimes you can that happened within, say, a six month time frame before Mr. Doe found his new identity."

"That could be thousands," he said. "Counting New York it could be millions."

"Narrow it as best you can. Look for 'wanted's' that fit his general age and description. Start with felonies and work your way down. See if anything fits."

"Geez Louise, Maggie."

"It's called old-fashioned police work."

"It could take days."

"You got anything better to do?"

* * * *

The young man had left another paper bag outside her motel room door. She didn't answer when he knocked, but waited until the door slammed down the hall before opening her own and looking out. She picked up the bag then spun around, double locking the door behind her.

She plopped down on the bed, curious as to what his latest gift to her might be. On one level his game scared her, on another it was like opening presents on Christmas or her birthday.

When she reached inside the bag, her fingers felt something soft and fluffy. Slowly, she pulled it out, looking at it with puzzlement and confusion.

A sensation swelled and grew deep in her stomach as she stared at it. A feeling akin to emptiness—or longing—or something not quite remembered. She wondered why he had given her this old thing as she held it in her hands and studied it. Two black button eyes looked back at her. It was a brown teddy bear. She laughed at the small tear where it's nose had once been, loose threads hanging from its wound like make-believe boogers. It must have been a child's well-loved and cherished companion, as the fur was stained and the fabric was thread-bare where the child had carried it around by it's neck. Her body rocked back and forth as she clutched the bear against her chest, holding it tightly and comforting it.

"I'll call you Mr. Muggles," she whispered into its ragged ear. One lone tear traced a path down her cheek. "That's a good name, don't you think?"

She recognized his knock.

This time she opened it, just a crack.

"It's time we talked," he said.

"I don't know you."

"You do. But you might not remember me. I'm David."

At first it meant nothing to her. David. David. But his name held the same vague familiarity she felt when she'd decided to call the teddy bear Mr. Muggles.

"My name is Darlene."

"No, your name is Darla."

Reluctantly, she let him in.

They talked for a long time. After he left, he dialed a long distance number.

"I'll make a reservation for a red eye flight that'll have you here tomorrow," he said. "I think she's ready. I'll email you the ticket info and boarding passes. When you get here take a taxi to the address I'm sending you."

There was a pause as he listened to the voice at the other end.

"No. I don't want her out of my sight. Do it my way. When you get here go to Room Twelve. I'll be waiting."

At the same time he was on the phone, the girl was dialing the number on Maggie Reardon's business card.

"I need your help," she sobbed. "My…husband…is missing."

* * * *

The loud afternoon sun screamed across the car's windshield, temporarily blinding Maggie Reardon as she turned west onto Miracle

Mile. She was heading for the Pink Flamingo Motel. The *Mary Smith* girl, the one who had made the series of 911 disconnects, had refused to come to the police department to file a missing persons report. That was odd enough in itself. Then she'd said she wasn't supposed to leave her room, which struck Maggie as even stranger. If her husband's disappearing act was important, you'd think she'd be down there in a New York minute. It could be nothing more than a man out on a binge and Maggie could have written it off right there. Oddballs were everywhere and there was no crime in that. But something hadn't felt right. Her curiosity was getting the best of her. She'd known the woman was lying. The what and why of it begged answers. If the young woman wouldn't come to Maggie then Maggie would go to her.

It was time to fill in some blanks.

* * * *

Maggie's conversation with the young woman was as strange as their first. And as guarded. She had finally confessed that her name was Darlene rather than Mary, but even that tidbit changed from Darlene to Darla and then back again. And she damn near panicked when Maggie asked her for her last name. It was as if she didn't know. Or was afraid to give the true answer. The woman clutched a bag of animal cookies and nibbled on them nervously every time Maggie asked a question. She was as skittish as a feral cat and twice as wary. Maggie sensed that if she pushed too hard Darlene would stop talking altogether. She needed to rein in her impatience and gain the woman's trust. A little information was better than none at all. At least for now.

Darlene had tossed the empty animal cookie bag into the wastebasket and replaced it with a worn out teddy bear, clutching it close. The most she was able to get out of her was a physical description of her missing husband, whose name also seemed to have escaped her.

His description sounded familiar.

He sounded a hell of a lot like her John Doe from the Arizona-Sonoran Desert Museum who had been removed from his cactus bed only to take up residence on a cold slab in the morgue.

But Maggie didn't tell her that. She had the impression that Darlene was too fragile to digest it in one big dose. Instead Maggie wrote in her notepad, jotting down what little information Darlene provided. She'd have to get a few head shots of the man they found in the javelina enclosure and hope that Darla/Darlene could handle it when she had her identify the body from the photos.

They could take her in for questioning after that, whether she liked it or not.

There was also the chance that she was trying to cover up. If she and the man down the hall were lovers, one of them could be the killer. It's not rare that the first person who offers assistance in an investigation is the perpetrator. They think their cooperation removes them from the suspect list, but more often than not the opposite is true.

"I'll get back to you," she'd said reassuringly.

She'd need to work through this in baby steps.

CHAPTER FIFTEEN

Nightmares

When Maggie returned to the office, Aaron Iverson was sitting at the desk next to hers sifting through a shoulder-high stack of print-outs. She almost felt guilty saddling him with such a tedious task. Almost. It was better than his being on temporary leave with nothing to do but replay Jerry Montana's actions over and over in his head, second-guessing his own performance between trips to the department shrink. She told herself she was doing him a favor, but she was doing herself a bigger one. She liked the action on the street. It made her feel alive. Being hunched over a computer or filling out reports was as much fun as a windowless room full of accountants juggling numbers in their claustrophobic cubicles.

Like she'd told Rocco, she needed air.

And elbow room.

"How's it coming?" she asked.

"Frustrating." He said he was narrowing them down by time frame, description, and state. The wastepaper basket was overflowing, but there was a secondary stack of reports next to the taller pile that he said was half-way promising and worth a second look.

"Frazzled?"

"You betcha, Detective Reardon. My eyes feel like a John Deere yanked them right out of their sockets."

"Then let's call it a day."

He wore a bloodshot expression of relief, followed by a weak thank you. He needn't know it was primarily because she wanted to feed her cat and take a hot shower. And that Italian dinner Rocco La Crosse had promised. She'd been so caught up in her work that she'd forgotten to eat. Caffeine and nicotine and the occasional hit of adrenaline could carry her just so far. She was getting hungry.

Maggie hoped that her second official date with Rocco would be as good as the first one. Maybe that initial rush was as good as it gets, that had proven true in the past. But she'd prefer it was a harbinger of better things to come.

Was there anything that could top the first time with a new lover, let alone match it?

Only time would tell.

* * * *

Maggie sat in her father's overstuffed chair, basking in the after-glow of her second date with Rocco La Crosse. Prowler sat on her lap, admonishing her with soft growls. She felt bad leaving him alone so much, so she consoled him with chin rubs and scratched him on the spot where his tail met his back. He always liked that. It was the one spot he was unable to reach himself. His tongue darted in and out like he was having a seizure and his back rose high as she scratched him toward his feline ecstacy. He purred. Men and cats. They could be easy and they could be impossible.

* * * *

The meal Rocco had prepared on their first date was great, but the Italian food they'd shared tonight was even better. And the big bottle of Chianti they'd polished off wasn't bad either.

She'd taken the alpha role again, leading him straight to the bed-room before their dinner had a chance to settle. If the first night had been a violin solo by Itzak Perlman, then tonight was the entire Philhar-monic Orchestra playing the 1812 Overture. Their first time had been wonderful, no argument there, but they'd been cautious, careful not to overstep some unknown, invisible boundary. This time their kisses were filled with anticipation as they explored new territory. They found each others perfect spots and spiked their intensity by sizzling degrees. Afterwards they collapsed, exhausted and comfortable. It didn't bother him when she'd dressed and headed for home rather than falling asleep against his chest as she'd done the first time.

Perfect.

Like a good book, the night had a beginning, a middle and an end.

Prowler jumped off her lap, his paws padding softly across the floor as he headed to the bedroom, determined to get the best spot on the mattress before his mistress joined him. Maggie looked around the living room, at all the decorations and mementos and stacks of dusty books that had been there since she was a child. Nothing had been changed. Nothing. It was as if she'd preserved it as a permanent shrine to her parent's memory.

Jerry Montana.

He just woke up from where he'd been sleeping in that uncomfortable corner of her brain and gave her a nasty kick. Was she just as trapped in the past as he had been? Were her surroundings an indication that she was in danger of slipping down that same, dark hole? Well, she wasn't about to let that happen.

"Snap out of it, Maggie," she ordered herself. "It's time for the present."

Thrift stores were out there for good reason. They were places to let go of the past. Tomorrow she'd get boxes and start packing things up. It was time to see these possessions for what they were. They were memories, not her parents. She didn't need to be surrounded by them to hold on to those memories. The chair in which she sat was too comfortable to give up, but she could have it re-upholstered. Her mother's small jewelry box and its contents were treasures that would stay right where they were. But they'd be in perspective rather than taking front stage. Everything else could slip back into its own decade, to be rediscovered by someone walking down the aisles of the second-hand store discovering them for the first time.

It was the sane thing to do.

Jerry Montana's loss had killed him long before he'd killed himself.

She could almost hear her parents applauding from above. Or from wherever people go once their time on earth is finished. Their time was behind them and hers was ahead of her. It didn't mean she loved them any less.

She would repaint the walls. In cheerful colors. And pull down the heavy drapes that covered the windows leaving a dark pall. It was time for the house to be happy again.

"Let there be light," she said as she rose and headed for the bedroom.

No way in hell was she going to end up like Jerry Montana.

She slid under the covers and was asleep by the time her head hit the pillow.

In the middle of the night she awoke to a loud, metallic clanking from outside the bedroom walls. Was somebody trying to remove the wrought iron bars at her window? Her heartbeat increased along with the racket. Clank, clank, clank. She threw back the covers and reached for the handgun on her night stand. Home invasions were no stranger to Tucson.

Clank.

Thud. Thud. Thump.

Gun in hand, she tiptoed out of the bedroom, through the living room and kitchen and unlocked the back door without making a sound. If someone was looking for trouble, then Maggie Reardon was ready to meet them head on. She followed the sound as she edged slowly along the side of the house and peered around the corner. The big, metal swamp cooler stood like a metallic sentinel, lit faintly by the moonlight and surrounded by awkwardly moving shadows.

Javelinas.

She'd forgotten to close the gate.

Their sense of smell was impressive. A family of them were throwing their bodies against the metal walls of the cooler, then rooting impatiently where it kissed the ground, frantic to get to the water inside. Water was scarce in the desert and they thought they'd found their treasure.

They were mistaken.

Maggie stomped her feet and yelled, "Shoo!"

A large boar turned to face her, snorting loudly and shifting his weight from one foot to another. Others joined him, huddling at his sides.

"Pose and threat all you want, mister. You might have tusks but I've got the gun. And it's loaded and ready. Now shoo before I start shooting! Shoo, shoo, shoo!"

He stomped his feet and Maggie stomped hers.

She continued her threatening dance, waving her arms high above her head while growling at them.

A few more snorts, squeals and stomps before they turned and ran. They had an odd arthritic-like gait, walking stiffly as if they had no knees. The snorting and squealing was slowly swallowed by the night.

Maggie latched the gate then returned to her bedroom.

Sleep was disturbing and intermittent. Dreams drifted in and out between the dark nothingness of deep slumber.

Dismembered arms reached out from clusters of cacti, their gnarled fingers raking furrows along the dusty ground. The Book of Mormon did battle with a bible and Koran while Madeline Murray O'Hare looked on, laughing from where she stood in the shadows. Julie London sang "The Thrill is Gone" and Alex Trebek led the orchestra while bright pink animal crackers danced to the tune. Rocco La Crosse stood naked in the desert, arms reaching upward toward the heavens like a canonized saint and the dry arroyos ran red with blood.

She was relieved when daylight came.

CHAPTER SIXTEEN

So, Who's the Bad Guy?

"I want Iverson with me," Maggie said to the Captain.

"He's desk-bound. Period."

"I'm close to giving our John Doe a name," she said, holding the morgue shots of alias Delbert Frimel. "I'm going to question the girl again. And show her the photos. I think he's her missing husband."

"Why the photos? Why not just bring her in to I.D. him?"

"She's scared. She refuses to leave her room."

"So drag her in."

"I can get more this way. At least for now."

"So why do you need the rookie along?"

"A male officer gets more respect. Sad but true, but it will give her the message we mean business. He's good backup and I trust him more than I ever trusted Jerry Montana."

"Maggie, if you think the situation might be dangerous…"

"No, she's just a scared little rabbit. But a good scout is always prepared."

"The last thing we need is another headline."

"Cop catches rabbit? I doubt it would make front page."

The two of them went back and forth and back again. Maggie wasn't about to give up and the Captain was weakening.

"You're annoying," he said. "Go ahead and take the kid with you. Now get out of here and don't you dare make any more trouble for me than I already have."

* * * *

The weather couldn't make up its mind. Dark clouds were building up in the distance, again threatening rain. Once it reached Tucson it could give birth to anything from a few drops to spike the humidity or a full-blown downpour to wash pick-up trucks into ravines. Either way, it was getting ready to do something. It was just a matter of when and what.

Maggie Reardon and Aaron Iverson were parked in the lot of the Pink Flamingo Motel. Maggie wore street clothes with her badge as a necklace. Aaron sat next to her looking official with his flashy badge pinned to his uniform. She filled him in on yesterday's encounter with Darlene. Earlier they had observed the young man from down the hall enter her room. Even if he was just for window dressing, Maggie was glad she'd brought Aaron along. Almost as glad as he was to be rescued from the computer.

"When we go in, stand there looking tough," she said. "And watch my back. I don't know what to expect when she sees these pictures but I'm positive, no almost positive, that she holds the key. The description was spot on."

A taxi pulled into the space next to them. A woman with grey streaks in her hair, who looked just on the kinder side of fifty, got out and paid the driver. She wore practical shoes and her plain green house dress clashed with her bloodshot eyes. She held one small carry-on suitcase that looked like it was making its first trip. The taxi left, but instead of heading to check-in she stood looking at the building. Her eyes scanned the doors until they landed on the one she was searching for. She inhaled deeply and squared her shoulders, then headed straight for Room Twelve.

Aaron reached for the door handle and Maggie stopped him.

"Let's sit tight," she said.

The woman knocked on the door. It was opened by the young man. He took her suitcase, ushered her in, slammed the door shut.

"Surprise," said Aaron. "If those two are lovers, then what's a middle-aged woman doing in the mix? She doesn't smell like a drug dealer, that's for sure."

"And an unlikely choice for a threesome. It's getting interesting, don't you think?"

The two sat for several more minutes, then exited the car.

Their knocks on the door of Room Twelve went unanswered.

Aaron knocked again, this time harder.

The young man opened the door. He wore Levi's. His blue shirt pocket held a glass case and a pencil. He also wore a look of surprise mixed with suspicion.

"We don't want any," he said rudely, attempting to shut the door. Maggie blocked it with her foot like a Fuller Brush Man refusing to take no for an answer.

"A few questions," said Aaron.

"You're unwanted here."

"You might find *here* more comfortable. Maybe not. Our interrogation room is better lit."

He held the door as the two officers entered. Darlene sat in her usual spot in the middle of the bed, staring at the blank television screen. It was as if she wasn't there, oblivious to her surroundings and the people who filled the room. She didn't look up, just sat there staring at nothing and clutching a ragged teddy bear.

"There's nothing we can't handle ourselves," said the older woman. Maggie looked into her stern eyes. They were the identical shade of blue as Darlene's. As well as the young man's. How had she not noticed that they shared the same features? Interchangeable noses and eyes and hair color. The family resemblance was a dead giveaway.

"My sister isn't up to talking," he said.

"What's your name?" asked Maggie.

"David," he said. "I'm David Fitzgerald."

"Fitzgerald," whispered Darlene (or was it Darla?) "Fitzgerald. Fitz. Fitz. Fitz."

"And I'm Mrs. Fitzgerald. Louise. I'm their mother and this is family business. We don't need strangers sticking their noses where they don't belong."

"Delbert Frimel. Does that ring a bell?" asked Maggie.

The mother and son looked confusedly at each other, then shrugged.

"Del," said Darlene, never taking her eyes off the televison. "Del."

They were like watching a clan of brainless, stumbling zombies.

"Darla," said David. "Everything's okay now."

The mother crossed the room and sat on the bed next to her daughter, putting her arm around her shoulder and pulling her close. "I never thought I'd see you again, baby. I'm here now and you're safe."

There was no reaction from her daughter.

"You're breaking my heart, Darla. You're just breaking your mother's heart."

Maggie slid the morgue photos from their envelope and handed them to the brother. She was afraid if Darla saw them first the room might explode. He looked, then tossed them onto the floor.

"Does he look familiar?"

"Yea, I know him," he sneered.

"Well?"

The mother looked at one of the upturned photos that had landed on the floor near the bed, let out a derisive snort, then interrupted.

"As soon as he was old enough to get a driver's license, David left in search of his sister. He never gave up. His heart told him she was alive. That she was out there somewhere and he was determined to find her. David loves his little Darla. It damn near broke our hearts when she went missing."

"She didn't go missing Mama, she was stolen. Go ahead, tell them."

"Some things are too shameful to put words to."

"It's time," said Maggie.

"I opened her bedroom door and I caught him dead to rights."

"Go on."

"I ran out of the room. I was dialing the police when he hit me over the head with something. By the time I came to he was gone. And he'd taken Darla with him."

"The police never found them, but I suspect they didn't look very hard." David started pacing the small room. "It was her father that took her, not a stranger. And women make those accusations sometimes, just to get the upper hand, you know? I don't think they took it seriously. He was her father and you can't really steal your own flesh and blood."

"His real name?" asked Aaron.

"Don. Don Fitzgerald."

"Now we're getting somewhere."

"I've been searching for years, but they were always one step ahead. Dear old dad talked about California sunshine a lot, so I figured they headed west. He always hated Vermont winters, but I don't know anybody that likes snow, do you? At least here you don't have to shovel the sunshine. You're lucky." He paused to take a breath. "Do you know the first thing she said to me once I convinced her I was her brother? She'd forgotten she even had one. She said that I must be married to Mama now. Can you imagine? How freakin' twisted is that? My father had told her that when little girls grew up they married their daddies and little boys grew up to marry their mommies. Hell, she was only seven when he took her. God only knows how long things had been going on before that. He painted her with his own ugly filth. He brainwashed her until she didn't know anything except what he told her."

"My husband is missing," said Darla.

"Just stop it, Darla," said David. "He's not your husband!"

Darla looked over at the photos that were strewn across the floor. She sat upward, dropping her teddy bear as she jumped over her mother and fell to the floor. She grasped one of the photos and stared at it, then held it closer to her heart than she'd been holding the teddy bear.

"Del? Is that my Del?"

"He's better off gone," said the mother.

"You're lying," she said, crawling back onto the center of the bed. Her mother reached for her. "Don't touch me! Del told me the world is full of danger and liars and I should only trust him. He protected me. He loved me, he said so."

"He was the liar, Darla. He filled your head with lies. I love you the real way."

"My husband loves me!" she said to her mother. Then looking up at her brother, "Are you the monster? Are you the one who did this to him?"

"I love you. I set you free." H glanced at the cops then took a self-protective step backwards. There wasn't far to go in that small room without hitting a wall.

"Liars, you're both liars," she screamed. Then something flipped a switch behind her eyes and they went dark. She reached over and picked up the remote from the night stand and pressed the button. "It's time for cartoons now," she said, as if the events of the past several minutes had never happened.

"David, we need to go downtown," said Maggie.

He took another backwards step.

"No," he said. "I have to stay with Darla."

He reached into the pocketed glass case and pulled something out. Quicker than a flash he charged Maggie, his arm held over his head like Tony Perkins in the shower scene from Psycho. She tried to block him as he stabbed downward with the ice pick. It missed it's mark but not before it tore across her shoulder, ripping through her blouse and drawing blood. She lunged forward, throwing him off balance and knocking him to the ground. Aaron flew across the room and joined the tackle. He knelt next to her, cuffing a struggling David as Maggie held him down full weight.

"Looks like we found our killer," she said. "And the murder weapon is our bonus." She and Aaron hoisted David to a standing position. Aaron pushed him against the wall and Maggie pulled a clear plastic bag out of her pocket, using a tissue to lift the ice pick and drop it into the bag. "And I'll bet that traces of Daddy Fitzgerald's blood are still on it."

"You can't tell me he didn't deserve what he got," said David.

Maggie Reardon was hard put to disagree with him.

"You're bleeding, Maggie," said Aaron.

"I'll put a band-aid on it later."

"You're gonna need more than a band-aid."

By now the mother had risen from the bed and stood before them, feet planted firmly on the dingy carpet.

"You can't take him," she said. "You can't take my baby."

Aaron Iverson was reading David his Miranda Rights as he led him towards the door.

"Do you understand your right to remain silent?" asked Aaron.

But David Fitzgerald kept right on talking. He told them he was justified in shoving that ice pick into his father's ear and tossing his body into the javelina enclosure. He said he'd have done worse if he could have. His little sister was hurt and the punishment fit the crime. He offered no regrets and no apologies and Maggie didn't blame him, not one bit. Once again she found herself drifting into that grey area that lived somewhere between right and wrong. But this time she refused to get involved. This time she'd listen to the Captain's advice. She was a cop, not a social worker. Her job was to apprehend him and book him. The rest was up to judge and jury. The victim was more of a bad guy than the one she was hauling off to jail. Next time she wanted to collar a guy who was bad to the bone. Erasing those grey areas would make her job easier.

Darla sat in bed, her focus on the cartoons, oblivious to the drama unfolding before her.

"I just found my one baby. I can't lose the other one," the mother begged. "Please, please don't take him. Don't do this to us. Haven't we been through enough?"

Darla looked up at the detective.

"My husband is missing," she said. "Will you help me find him?" She picked up the remote, turned her attention to the cartoons and jacked up the volume.

"I'm sorry, Mrs. Fitzgerald, but right now there's a seven-year-old girl who's in desperate need of your help." Maggie handed Mrs. Fitzgerald her card. "You can find us here."

The woman stood silent as Maggie Reardon and Aaron Iverson walked through the door with her only son. She watched through the motel room window as they shoved him into the back seat of their car and drove away. A few drops of rain made a crooked pattern as they hit the glass and slid down the motel room window. The pattern repeated itself as salty tears quietly fell from Mrs. Fitzgerald's eyes and down her aging face. Woody Woodpecker was laughing. Then a commercial came on. An ad for sugar coated breakfast cereal with a happy cartoon face on the box. She walked over to the dresser and picked up the fresh bag of animal cookies that David had brought for his sister. She sat down on the bed next to her little girl and tore it open, holding it in front of her as if it were a peace offering.

"I should have known, but I didn't. And I'm sorry," she said. "Here sweetheart, why don't you have a few of these? You must be getting hungry."

Darla reached into the bag, removed a handful of pink and white cookies and ate them one by one, saving the white ones for last, just as she'd always done. She picked up Mr. Muggles, holding the teddy bear close as she turned off the television and inched her body down the mattress. She hesitated, then lay her head on her mother's lap.

"It's time for my nap now," she said.

And she fell asleep.

CHAPTER SEVENTEEN

Haven

It had taken some coaxing, but Maggie Reardon convinced Carlos to join her for a night out. He'd spent his life in the mini-mart long enough and his nephew was more than willing to hold down the fort in his absence. Gentleman that he was, Carlos had insisted on picking her up at her front door. They arrived at The Mosaic Gallery arm in arm. What better place for the public debut of her friend Carlos and his shiny new teeth? It was reception night.

And it was Barbara Atwell's welcome home.

The gallery rooms were packed with familiar faces as well as new ones. Some came out of loyalty, others out of curiosity, but the results were the same. Sales were flying off the walls and an air of excitement filled the rooms. The first thing that caught her eye was a large abstract in shades of white on white. There was no mistaking that the artist was Misty Waters, the rape victim to whom she'd suggested contacting The Center Against Sexual Assault. But there was something different about her painting this time. In the upper right corner was a splash of color. A washed out soft blue, but it was color. Standing next to it, the normally introverted Misty was smiling and talking, wrapped in her usual monochromatic whites but with a pale blue flower in her hair and a touch of blue eye shadow. She had taken Maggie's advice and the counseling already showed results. She was healing, one cautious color at a time. Their eyes met and Misty mouthed the words *thank you.* Maggie nodded, then ushered Carlos deeper into the room, introducing him to the artists and pointing out their works. He immediately focused on a bold collage. Calypso, the belly-dancing artist, shimmied her way across the room towards them smelling a potential sale. She wiggled up to them, standing out from the crowd in her usual gypsy costume of brightly clashing colors and clanking jewelry.

"Do you like it?" she asked.

"Yes, they are the happy colors of Mexico at fiesta time," said Carlos.

The compliment made her shine. But as usual, her attention quickly faltered.

"Misty gave me the bird," she said to Maggie.

"Well, that was certainly impolite," said a voice from behind them.

"No, she didn't flip me the bird. She gave me the bird. Baretta."

"That foul-mouthed cockatoo?"

Maggie smelled the aroma of Blue Waltz perfume mixed with the faintest hint of stale marijuana smoke and knew who'd be standing there when she turned around.

"We really need to get together for another cup of tea," said the elderly and beautiful Mary Rose, "but first you must introduce me to your friend."

Carlos and Mary Rose couldn't take their eyes off each other. The old romance magnets were pulling full force. She'd never thought of Carlos that way before. Never considered him in any light other than father and friend. It was looking as if the life his nephew had so subtly suggested was ready to burst into bloom.

"I thought you and Rocco were an item," said Mary Rose.

"We are. Carlos and I are friends."

"Good news in more ways than one."

Carlos flashed his best smile.

"Where have you been hiding him, my dear? My God, he's as handsome and dashing as the actor Gilbert Roland."

Maggie left them to flirt with each other.

She congratulated Rocco and a glowing Adrian on their success. They stood next to the statuesque Barbara Atwell with her perfectly-coifed blonde hair as she held court with the well-wishers anxious to welcome her back. Her smile was as elegant as her classic dress. She leaned over and hugged Adrian, happy to be home where she belonged. After Montana's suicide and putting together the tragic puzzle surrounding the corpse at the Desert Museum, Maggie was ready for a happy ending.

And this was it.

A Tucson cop and a group of eccentric artists made for strange bedfellows, yet The Mosaic Gallery had become her haven. Were it not for the unfortunate circumstance that had first brought her here, she would never have met Rocco La Crosse. Or Mary Rose. Or any of the other people that she now considered friends. Amazing how a dead man on a gallery floor could serve as a positive catalyst. And Barbara's expression made it clear she held no animosity toward her for doing her job.

In the end, everything worked out for the best.

She wove her way through the crowd, studying the new art on the walls and shelves. Bold colors, muted tones, abstracts and landscapes. And naughty metal statues by Rocco La Crosse. There was jewelry, there were ceramics, and there was warmth mixed with an aura of optimism. It was breathing life and beauty and shining light onto a world that sometimes slipped into the darkness.

It was a place filled with hope.

Mary Rose walked up to her.

"It's a good show."

"It's perfect," said Maggie.

"Your friend is delicious. And such a gentleman. Too good of a gentleman, really."

"Is there such a thing?"

"I asked him over for a cup of tea," she said with a wink, "but he said that he was your escort and obligated to drive you home."

From across the room Maggie could see Carlos looking at Mary Rose with the adoration of a leading man in a romantic movie. Or a cocker spaniel puppy. She couldn't help but smile. One was never too old for love and tonight there was plenty to go around.

"Tell your Romeo I'll find another way home," she said, then added: "and don't be corrupting him with those funny cigarettes."

"Oh, I'll take good care of him, my dear. I promise."

Detective Maggie Reardon walked over to Rocco and whispered in his ear.

"Your place or mine?" he asked.

"They say one always returns to the scene of the crime."

"Then my place it is."

ABOUT THE AUTHOR

Lonni Lees is a multi-award winning writer. Her stories have appeared in *Hardboiled Magazine* and the anthologies *Deadly Dames*, *More Whodunits*, *Battling Boxing Stories*, and *Felons, Flames And Ambulance Rides* and online on Yellow Mama, A Shot of Ink, Shotgun Honey, Black Petals, All Due Respect and others. Her first short story collection, *Crawlspace*, her novels, *Deranged* (which won the PSWA 2012 award for Best Published Novel) and *The Mosiac Murder*, a Maggie Reardon Mystery, are available from Wildside Press. She lives in Arizona with her scientist husband and shows her art at a Tucson gallery.

www.ingramcontent.com/pod-product-compliance
Lightning Source LLC
Chambersburg PA
CBHW020144180626
46810CB00004B/1726